"*The Red-Headed Pilgrim* illum. what it means to search for meaning and beauty in this world. With quick wit and refreshing humor, Maloney has crafted a coming of age and adulthood story that exposes the gritty underside of idealization without losing all hope. This book was a wild, exuberant ride."
—**MADELINE HAUSMANN, BOOKPEOPLE (AUSTIN, TX)**

"Just as life does over and over again to its hero, Kevin Maloney's *The Red-Headed Pilgrim* knocked me down, picked me up, tickled my ribs, knocked me down again, kicked sand in my face, made my bed in the dirt, and then rubbed my back. It's John Williams by way of Sam Lipsyte, and it's not to be missed."
—**GREG KORNBLUH, DOWNBOUND BOOKS (CINCINNATI, OH)**

"A very funny and rollicking novel about one young man's often ill-fated quest for authenticity, originality, and beauty in modern times. Part of a generation raised in relative privilege by tv and breakfast cereal, he seeks more than the cog in the machine 9-5 life expected of him in search of unique experience, be it through farming, retail, travel, sex, drugs, rock and roll, all the way to marriage and fatherhood, often falling flat on his face. I devoured this book in one evening and enjoyed his misadventures thoroughly."
—**SETH TUCKER, CARMICHAEL'S BOOKSTORE (LOUISVILLE, KY)**

"Looking back at young mistakes from middle-age is a time-honored tradition. Especially for those who've harbored artistic or utopian dreams (or delusions, as the case may be.) Maloney doesn't give us the wish-fulfillment ending by having Kevin quit his comfortable job and go back on the road to sound his barbaric yawp, but neither does he close the door on the possibility that some pie-in-the-sky hopes may still come true."
—**DMITRY SAMAROV, *NEUTRAL SPACES***

"There are pages in here where every.single.sentence is funny."
—JOE WALTERS, *INDEPENDENT BOOK REVIEW*

"It's such a goddamn gem of a novel that I can't help but get swept up in the story of Kevin Maloney: poet, Buddhist, 'shroom-tripper, aloof charmer."
—GENE KWAK, AUTHOR OF *GO HOME, RICKY!*

"Unfailingly affable, often hilarious, sometimes harrowing, *The Red-Headed Pilgrim* is a künstlerroman—a novel detailing a young person's development into an artist—that tells the tale of one tall, white, Boho-American male's staggering path to creative fulfillment. With many detours through the swamps of sex, drugs, farm work, and fatherhood along the way, this novel is filled with deceptively hard-won wisdom, all wrapped in a brightly-colored bow."
—JON RAYMOND, AUTHOR OF *FREEBIRD*

"The author maintains a sharp wit and a knack for bringing zany flare to everyday details in his protagonist's awkward quest to build a life, and the author's willingness to get laughs at his narrator-doppelgänger's expense makes for a good use of the form. This funny and open-hearted romp will have readers laughing and reflecting on their own misadventures and foibles."
—*PUBLISHERS WEEKLY*

"I devoured this book. What a beautiful ode to being a fucked up pathetic virgin. *The Red-Headed Pilgrim* is intimate and vulnerable and sexy in the most raw, uncomfortable, depressing ways. Kevin Maloney, through years of poor decisions and contradictory impulses, shows us what he seemed to always know: there is nothing more powerful than love."
—CHELSEA MARTIN, AUTHOR OF *TELL ME I'M AN ARTIST*

"A revelation that achieves starry dynamo-level energy from the jump. Maloney's prose is sharp and vivid, full of trippy precision, and his story is funny, wild, painful and wise. When the road of *On the Road* runs into shattered middle age, this book is waiting for you."
—**SAM LIPSYTE, AUTHOR OF *HARK* AND *THE ASK***

"A fascinating novel about what can happen when you pursue beauty above all else. Money, reality, and corporate jobs are the last thing on this narrator's mind—instead, he'll go wherever love takes him. Kevin Maloney's writing will break your heart in the best way, reminding us how difficult life can be when we follow the path towards meaning, understanding, and belonging."
—**CHELSEA HODSON, AUTHOR OF *TONIGHT I'M SOMEONE ELSE***

"A funny, raw, eccentric novel that made me laugh out loud frequently as I tore through its pages. What I appreciated most about this bittersweet, darkly comic story, though, is how it is tinged so beautifully with hope in the end."
—**JAMI ATTENBERG, BESTSELLING AUTHOR OF *THE MIDDLESTEINS* AND *ALL GROWN UP***

"Who doesn't love a good disaster story, told with humor and good grace? ...The main character has hints of those old-school hapless heroes from the pages of Salinger or Brautigan, with a dash of modern day love-able losers like, say, *Napoleon Dynamite*. It's a drug and sex fueled *Odyssey*, with way less violence and death, and hardly any monsters, come to think of it. But I believe you'll enjoy it all the same."
—**ARTHUR BRADFORD, AUTHOR OF *TURTLEFACE AND BEYOND***

"Kevin Maloney has lovingly shoved the great American novel into a tank of LSD and it's crawled out with triumphant stars in its eyes. *The Red-Headed Pilgrim* is a beautifully melted comic work with a profound and eternal heart."
—**BUD SMITH, AUTHOR OF *TEENAGER***

Also by Kevin Maloney

Cult of Loretta
Horse Girl Fever

The
Red-Headed
Pilgrim

Kevin Maloney

a novel

Two Dollar Radio
Books too loud to ignore

Two Dollar Radio
Books too loud to Ignore

WHO WE ARE Two Dollar Radio is a family-run outfit dedicated to reaffirming the cultural and artistic spirit of the publishing industry. We aim to do this by presenting bold works of literary merit, each book, individually and collectively, providing a sonic progression that we believe to be too loud to ignore.

TwoDollarRadio.com

Proudly based in
Columbus
OHIO

 @TwoDollarRadio

@TwoDollarRadio

/TwoDollarRadio

Love the
PLANET?
So do we.

Printed on Rolland Enviro.
This paper contains 100% post-consumer fiber,
is manufactured using renewable energy - Biogas
and processed chlorine free.

100%

PCF

PERMANENT

Printed in Canada

SOME RECOMMENDED LOCATIONS FOR READING:
At a bar, in the bath, with a cat on your lap, on a bus headed east or west, or pretty much anywhere because books are portable and the perfect technology!

AUTHOR PHOTO→ Courtesy of the author

COVER PHOTO→ Photo by @girlwithredhat on Unsplash
DESIGN→ Eric Obenauf

Editor: Eric Obenauf; Copyeditor: Asia Atuah

Two Dollar Radio acknowledges that the land where we live and work is the contemporary territory of multiple Indigenous Nations.

For Fennel

In my case Pilgrim's Progress consisted in my having to climb down a thousand ladders until I could reach out my hand to the little clod of earth that I am.

—Carl Jung

The
Red-Headed
Pilgrim

Prologue

Twelve years ago, I broke the only promise I ever made to myself: never to become one of *them*—an automaton, a cubicle puppet, an office worker. It was easy. In a moment of weakness masquerading as adulthood, I took my dad up on an offer he'd been making for years. He called up his fishing buddy, Dan Connell, who owns a marketing-PR firm in the suburbs of Portland. There was an interview, a formality. The following Monday I was sitting in a 6-by-6 cubicle, wearing a dress shirt from Target, trying to convince the 18-year-old version of myself—who once had an hour-long conversation with the ghost of Walt Whitman on a Robitussin-induced spirit journey—that despite all appearances, I was *singing the body electric* and *sounding my barbaric yawp over the roofs of the world.*

My plan, if I remember right, was to stick around for a month or two, just long enough to get my finances in order. Then, I don't know. Join a monastery. Buy a one-way ticket to Guatemala. Move to Taos and spend my days fabricating off-grid dwellings from old Michelins and empty wine bottles. That was the idea anyway, but every time I tried to put in my notice, my boss offered me a promotion, and before I knew it, a decade had passed.

Now I'm coming on 12 years—the average lifespan of a Golden Retriever—and all I can think about is cashing in my 401(k), buying a vintage trailer, and moving to the desert. Beginning, at 42, the life I should have been living all along: painting watercolors and writing novels among the cacti.

My workday begins at 9 a.m. with 258 unread messages in my inbox. The subject lines only barely resemble English: "SEO 101: Top 5 KPIs for Effective B2B Marketing." One promises to boost my search ranking using blog posts written by AI robots. Is this what God had in mind when He created the heavens, earth, minerals, rivers?

I fire off two or three productive-sounding emails and walk around the office. Nobody works, as far as I can tell. Trevor, the graphic designer, pretends to mock up ads in Photoshop while secretly playing video games in a tiny browser window. He just killed a cyborg with a flamethrower. Some days he wears a headset so he can talk to players in other parts of the country. Apparently they don't work either.

Most of my coworkers play solitaire. Liza prefers mahjong. Dave plays some kind of game where you have to keep farm animals alive. Me, I open Microsoft Word and tinker with my short stories, trying to dig meaning out of imaginary lives. "At least I'm writing," I tell myself. "That's almost the same thing as living."

At noon, my coworker Janet pops her head in my cubicle and says the website I've been working on has to go through one more round of updates and then we should be able to go live over the weekend. "You don't mind working over the weekend, do you?" she asks.

"That's fine," I say, but what I really mean is, "Behold the pissing away of a human life, Janet. I was going to spend Saturday extricating myself from the sinister forces lurking in this Dell computer, but on second thought that can wait."

Janet tries to talk to me about another client, but I'm either having heart palpitations or quietly losing my shit. I stand up and walk past her and go outside.

My company's building is one of a dozen in this business park. It's nondescript, intentionally. My boss's aesthetic is "make it look like everything else." I walk among the identical brick buildings, thinking about how I used to sit outside Ted's Coffeehouse in Beaverton, smoking cigarettes and making fun of guys like me.

Back then I had long red hair, but now I have medium-length red hair cut into a mullet. I'm trying to keep my integrity here in the business park. I want to be seen as a philosopher king despite all the evidence to the contrary.

My buddy Dylan predicted all of this back in 1997. We were coming down from a fear-inducing mushroom trip, the kind that takes you right to the edge. There were kittens everywhere. That was the summer Dylan smoked pot laced with PCP and drove around the suburbs from one pet store to the next, adopting as many of those fuzzy cherubs as they'd let him. Our brains were still firing exotic, complex thoughts, but mostly we were coming down, and we were covered in soft kittens.

It was Dylan who said, "I'm scared we're going to forget this."

"Forget what?" I asked.

"What do you think, man? This—" He waved his hand around, indicating air, molecules, kittens, the universe. "What if we forget everything and get jobs and turn into our fathers?"

I laughed. The idea was so fucking stupid. We obviously weren't going to turn into our fathers. It was just a matter of deciding whether we'd be poets or philosophers or painters, or whether we'd walk around for the rest of our lives, tripping out on beauty and giving food to the homeless.

"That's not going to happen," I said.

"You don't know that," said Dylan. "Think about the hippies. They all moved to the suburbs and bought minivans. One minute they're taking LSD and skinny-dipping in mud puddles, the next they're CEOs for a bunch of tech companies. It can happen to anyone."

I thought of the movie *Woodstock*—all those mangy teenagers in sandals standing around, goggle-eyed on acid, while Jimi Hendrix played "The Star-Spangled Banner" like he was inside a helicopter getting shot at by the Viet Cong.

When Jimi finished, everybody nodded and said, "Right on, brother!" They ate it up. The government told them to go to Vietnam, and they said, "Fuck you, Government." It was beautiful.

Then the '70s happened. The Bee Gees wore gold pants. Those same hippies took cocaine and got pregnant. Then it was all about the babies. Providing for them. House in the suburbs, Ford Aerostar, the evening commute. Goodbye, LSD.

For 12 years, the only thing that's kept my soul from shriveling up completely is that when it's slow, I take these long walks around the business park. The buildings look like Soviet-era prisons, but the firs and hemlocks are godly. They rise from the monotony, reaching brilliant green fingers to heaven. Near their peaks, red-tailed hawks fly in circles.

As a teenager I used to ride around in my mom's minivan, looking out the window, imagining what the world looked like before white people chopped down all the trees. One time—I couldn't help it—I turned to my mom and said, "Do you ever feel guilty that our ancestors committed genocide so we could have three Starbucks within a mile of our house?" My mom started crying and turned up the radio.

Later, we were at The Gap, shopping for school clothes. Instead of picking out a pair of jeans, I sat down on the hardwood floor and had a realization that I was going to die one day.

Whatever the distance is between shopping for a pair of jeans at The Gap with your mom and fathoming your own nothingness, that's my disease. From an early age it twisted me.

Past the Shriner's building, in a meadow grown over with Queen Anne's lace, I sit and think about how every single person on this planet will be a skeleton one day. There's no escape hatch, no pause button, no exemption for good behavior. Sooner or later Death shows up with his grab bag of diseases, saying, "Your turn next, buddy."

A pack of account managers in spandex zooms by, trying to squeeze in some cardio on their lunch break. The ones in back slow down, looking. They notice the office worker in the field without any shoes on. How long do I have to sit here before the local news shows up?

"AREA BUSINESSMAN SITTING IN GRASS FOR TWO WEEKS SPEAKS OF 'SEEING INTO THE ESSENCE OF THINGS'"

For the longest time I've felt hunted by death. The Big Blackness. I feel it coming every day. And the thing is—I'm not wrong.

I'm trying to find something permanent to hold on to, but there isn't anything. I used to hide under the dress shirt rack at The Gap. Now I'm hiding in an office. One day I'll hide in my grave.

This is the story of a pilgrim named Kevin Maloney. He leaves his home and everything he knows and goes looking for God. I'll tell you right now—he doesn't find Him. Either that or he finds Him everywhere. I'm still not sure.

I'm sitting in a field of Queen Anne's lace in a business park in the suburbs of Portland, Oregon. August 16, 2019. The trees rise from the monotony, reaching brilliant green fingers to heaven. One day I'll be dead and there won't be anything.

PART I
JOURNEY TO A DARK FOREST

1

Leave it to Beaverton

As a child in Beaverton, Oregon—a suburb of Portland the way the Monkees are a suburb of the Beatles—I was raised in front of the television, eating McDonald's every day, mainlining high fructose corn syrup, confused whether my real family was Mom, Dad, and my brother Pete, or *Mr. Belvedere*, *ALF*, and *The Golden Girls*. I was constantly stimulated. I had all my vaccination shots. Whenever I felt a vague desire for a peanut butter and jelly sandwich, somebody made me one. I should have turned out normal, but I didn't. What happened? Did I snack on lead paint chips as a baby? Did I play too close to the litter box and contract *Toxoplasma gondii*, a parasite associated with risk-taking, promiscuity, and schizophrenia?

For 14 years I was a robot. *Bleep bleep.* I accepted the world without question. My parents said, "There is a magical rabbit who brings chocolate on Easter, a holiday marking the day our dead god crawled out of his grave," and I said, "That makes sense." But in the fall of 1991, on the football field behind Tom Peterson High School, I suffered a psychological break that ripped me from my humdrum existence and caused me to fathom the permanent darkness that awaits us at the end of our lives.

It happened on a rainy Tuesday, halfway through an uneventful practice. I was standing on the sidelines, hiding behind the Gatorade cooler, trying to avoid the tackling drills my teammates were mindlessly engaged in. If it were up to me, I would have been at home playing video games, but my dad threatened to run over my Nintendo with a rototiller if I didn't follow in my brother's footsteps and join the JV football team.

Our coaches—three P.E. teachers with mustaches, all named Randy—were huddled together, discussing our recent 72-point loss to the Ramblin' Rod Bobcats. The problem, they decided, was that we were a bunch of sniveling cowards who'd never had the shit properly knocked out of us.

"All right, ladies," they said. "Put your Barbies away and line up—single file! Except you, Soldofsky. Here's a raw steak. Smell it. Smell the blood in there? Smells good, doesn't it? All these froshmen queers are full of that iron-rich liquid. Let's see if you can't spill some on this pretty green grass."

When the whistle blew, you were supposed to run at Kyle Soldofsky as fast as you could and try to tackle him. It was a joke. Until his recent DUI arrest, Kyle was an All-American tailback on a first-name basis with recruiters from Stanford and Notre Dame. We were nervous second-string punters hoping to survive on Planet Earth long enough to lose our virginities.

I was last in line, which gave me plenty of time to think about death. I didn't like it. I hadn't asked to be born, but now that I was here, I wanted to stick around for a while. Ideally, forever.

The whistle blew. Teenage bodies, delicate with barely fused bone plates, met horrible ends. Aaron Nowack emerged from a collision, holding a handful of teeth. Tom Boraz limped to the sidelines with a bone sticking out of him.

I didn't like either of those bastards. Once, in the showers, Tom put me in a headlock and made me drink an entire bottle of shampoo. Aaron was his lookout. Still, I didn't like watching all that blood gurgling out of them.

Eric McLemore made a courageous charge at Kyle and was rewarded with a seizure. Watching Eric die, I began to hallucinate. I saw the Grim Reaper sitting on the bleachers with his long sickle, making a "come here" gesture with his slender bone finger. I saw autumn leaves shimmering like gold coins, the bounty on our blood. I saw a lone crow wobbling around like a deranged undertaker preparing our caskets for the soil.

The whistle blew. Ben Varisano ran straight for Kyle. Kyle opened his mouth, ate Ben, and spit out his helmet. I ran for the forest.

It was dark. A squirrel saw me and scampered up the side of a tree. I didn't blame it; I would have done the same if I had sharp claws and a bushy tail.

In wartime, they shot deserters. My parents would do the same. They couldn't afford to have a philosopher in the family. I was a threat to their values, which consisted of doing everything they could for their son, who they sent onto a football field to be murdered by Kyle Soldofsky.

I sat on a log and looked up at the canopy of Douglas firs. Their limbs resembled the synapses of a magnificent green brain. I thought of my own brain: why was I so keen on preventing it from becoming permanently damaged? Why didn't I hurl myself at death like the other effeminate punters?

I popped the snap of my chinstrap, liberating my head from its protective armor. My hair flopped wet against my forehead. I started shivering. I didn't know if I was cold or scared. My entire life I'd been preparing to gleefully perish on a football field like my ancestors. I'd abandoned my sacred duty.

I started whimpering and thinking. Why was I born? Was there intelligence in nature? Did Jesus really walk the earth 2,000 years ago? Did He die for our sins?

I fell asleep in the fetal position. When I woke up, I was covered in dew. Walking home, my cleats clicked on the asphalt. The sound echoed off suburban houses, from which televisions glowed like intoxicating fireplaces.

My parents didn't kill me, but they sent me to a psychiatrist. His name was Dr. McClanahan. I sat on a gray couch next to a bookshelf and a bronze bust of John Lennon.

"Your parents tell me you're afraid of pain," said Dr. McClanahan.

"I don't like it," I admitted.

"Would you say you go out of your way to avoid it?"

"Oh yeah. If it were up to me, I'd experience pleasure all the time. Pleasure, yes. Pain, no."

He nodded and wrote something down. "And you say that in the forest you felt safe?"

"I felt like I wasn't going to die. Unless there were bears. I don't think there were bears."

Dr. McClanahan gestured toward the bronze bust. "Do you know who that is?"

"It's John Lennon," I said.

"It's the psychologist Carl Gustav Jung. He once said, 'A man is not what happens to him; he is what he chooses to become.' It's my belief that when you left the football field, you weren't running away from pain, you were embarking on a spiritual journey. In a sense, fear made you a pilgrim."

He went to his bookshelf and retrieved a slim paperback.

"I want you to read this," he said. "I think you'll get something out of it."

When I got home, I crawled into bed and started reading. It was *Siddhartha* by Hermann Hesse. It was about a boy who should have been happy but wasn't. One day he leaves his family and everything he knows and becomes a beggar who wanders around India, seeking enlightenment.

It was just like me, only my plan was to hide in my bedroom for the rest of my life, playing *Super Mario Bros.*

2

The Inevitable Death Society

Three years later, I'd grown my hair into a beautiful mane that flowed down my shoulders like a tangerine waterfall. For metaphysical reasons, I didn't play sports. If I went to a football game, it was only to smoke pot under the bleachers and gaze in agitation at the white thighs of cheerleaders who shook their pom-poms in the false light reflecting off a dozen trombones. I wasn't a good pilgrim. Mostly I smoked a lot of pot and spent all my time with other stoners who, like me, understood the secret of death. The secret was: HOLY SHIT I'M GOING TO DIE ONE DAY! ME! ALL OF THIS IS GOING TO END. FUCK!

While our classmates plotted their future careers with guidance counselors or guzzled wine coolers in the backseats of Buick LeSabres, we founded the Inevitable Death Society, an afterschool club for morbid 17-year-olds who didn't care about band or theater or chess since we were all going to be ashes eventually, permanently, for all of eternity.

Every Wednesday we gathered in an empty classroom behind the boiler room. The format resembled an A.A. meeting. We sat in a circle, staring at our hands, inside of which were bones, the seeds of our future skeletons, which would be licked clean by insects one day if some lazy-eyed mortician didn't jam us into a 2,000-degree oven first.

"Sometimes I wake up in the middle of the night and I'm so scared I want to jump out of my body," said Luke Janowski, a jittery freshman with a wardrobe comprised entirely of Nine Inch Nails t-shirts. "There's nowhere to go, man. This. All of it! FUCKING ALL OF IT! It's gonna be gone. FOREVER. ME!!!"

We nodded and said things like, "It doesn't make sense," and, "I get it, dude. I'm shaking right now."

We were a brotherhood of fear, united by our own impermanence and the frivolity of our sad suburban lives…

Until Laura showed up. She was looking for glee club and took a wrong turn and, for some reason, decided to stay. She was healthy, with a generally positive outlook on things. She didn't know the secret of death.

After a beautiful speech by Aaron Nowack on the subject of blood, the ridiculous red liquid whose movement momentarily separates us from the Chasm of Infinite Nothingness, Laura said, "All you guys talk about is *death death death*. It's depressing. Why don't you talk about something else for a change?"

She pulled a copy of *People* magazine out of her backpack and started reading it in front of us. There was a photograph of Johnny Depp on the cover. The caption read: "Love is a battle-field for Hollywood's talented, troubled young star."

Rather than scoff at the frivolous gossip surrounding so-called "celebrities," who pretended to be other people in exchange for money, here was our newest member scoffing at existentialism to read about the mating habits of Edward Scissorhands.

Laura licked her finger and turned the page defiantly. More than one of us fell in love with her.

I didn't believe in the objective reality of the homecoming dance, but I believed in sex, so I asked Laura to go with me. For two hours, we drank Sprite and slow-danced to Babyface and Boyz II Men. Then we went outside and sat on the concrete steps and laced our fingers together in an intricate manner that made it almost impossible to breathe.

There were stars scattered across the sky in erratic clusters resembling sea creatures and Roman gods.

I pointed and said, "I can't believe any of this exists. It would make way more sense if there was nothing at all."

Laura said, "You're so morbid. Why can't you just enjoy the time you have and not think about what comes next?"

I said, "What else is there to talk about?"

She said, "Lots of things."

I said, "Like what?"

She couldn't think of anything, so she put her tongue in my mouth.

I started shaking.

Laura said, "Are you okay?"

I wasn't sure if I was.

Laura got a chaperone to check on me.

The next day when I got to school, I heard a rumor that Laura was dating my best friend, Dylan. It was funny because I'd nearly died while making out with her the night before.

I went to Dylan's locker to tell him how funny it was and found him making out with Laura.

I said, "I don't understand. Why?"

Dylan said, "We're all going to die one day, brother. Nothing matters."

Dylan knew the secret of death.

I decided to commit suicide, so I went home and tied a rope around a ceiling joist and stood on a stool and lowered the noose over my head.

I was about to kick out the stool when I got a really good idea for a poem. It went:

I hate myself and want to die.
I hate myself and want to die.
I hate myself and want to die.
I hate myself and want to die.

I wrote it down on a piece of notebook paper and read it over and over. The poem was so good I could barely understand it. I'd always suspected I was a genius, and here was proof. I stayed up all night writing poems about how much I wanted to die and forgot to commit suicide.

The next day I told my English teacher that I was worried I might be a genius. I showed her my poems. She referred me to the guidance counselor, who referred me to Mr. Wensink, the hippie art teacher who had a framed photograph of Jerry Garcia on his desk.

I read him my poems.

He said, "That is some dope shit, Mr. Maloney. Any 17-year-old who doesn't want to commit suicide is a complete dud as far as I'm concerned. Have you read Richard Brautigan? He committed suicide, but first he wrote some beautiful poems."

He pulled a book off the shelf. It didn't have a title on the cover, just a photograph of a barefooted hippie woman crouching in a pile of rubble.

The book was full of poems about sex and penises and death and *machines of loving grace*. I read it, trembling, the slim volume tucked inside my geometry book while Mrs. Bell taught us the secret of solving polynomial equations. A few days later when I returned the book to Mr. Wensink, he loaned me *Naked Lunch* by William Burroughs. I started wearing a cape to school. Nobody was going to have sex with me anyway.

3

Mr. Pebbles

My friends applied to art school or dropped out and began careers in the funeral industry, the only vocation we considered real. I wanted to go to art school, but my parents pressured me into applying to the University of the Pacific Northwest, a private school in Tacoma, Washington, where my brother Pete was pursuing a degree in business. By some miracle having to do with the 4.0 GPA I'd maintained until I discovered the illicit joys of cannabis, they accepted me. My parents were overjoyed, but I wasn't sure I wanted to be alive on Planet Earth, let alone spend four years writing double-spaced essays about the role of specialization in promoting the efficiency of capital accumulation in Adam Smith's *The Wealth of Nations*.

Every day after school, instead of facing my parents, I hid in the forest behind the park, smoking pot out of a hollowed-out apple and gazing up into the forest canopy. The way I saw it, I was only going to be alive this one time. I didn't want to do what everyone else did. I imagined a different life—one where I spent my days outside, close to the earth, observing the serene movements of ladybugs. I wanted to notice the world—*really* notice it. To be arrested by it and conquered by it, and then I wanted to write a slim paperback that teenagers carried in their back pockets as they did drugs in the forest, trying to figure out what to do with their meaningless lives.

I took another hit and ate the apple. My heart beat frantically. I arose and walked. On drugs, the neighborhood I was born and raised in was too colorful. Goldfinches, bedecked in vibrant yellow feathers, shot across the sky, defying gravity. Lawns, mowed and fertilized, shone like emeralds. Rhododendrons went *bloop,* ejecting neon flowers out of their verdant branches.

The world was freaking me out, so I put on my Sony Walkman and listened to the Red Hot Chili Peppers on full blast. The songs were frenetic and had themes of sex and doing drugs in Los Angeles. Sometimes Anthony Kiedis felt like his only friend was the city he lived in.

"I know, Anthony," I said to a mailbox. "Believe me, I know."

Walking in no particular direction, I came upon my childhood friend Roy's house. I recalled the time he spent the night and got sad at 2 o'clock in the morning because he missed his gerbil, Mr. Pebbles. His mom had to come over and pick him up.

A gerbil! We were just boys then. In a few months, he would be studying anthropology at the University of Michigan.

At some point his parents, Tom and Debbie, planted shrubs in their yard. They were covered in flowers. The color was too bright. I shrieked and ran in the opposite direction.

A few days later Dylan called and said he'd scored a strain of weed called "Afghani Kill bud" that got you so stoned you hallucinated earthquakes. I was still mad at him for stealing my girlfriend, but I really wanted to know what an earthquake felt like, so I said, "Okay, rad."

I tiptoed downstairs, hoping to avoid my parents, but when I reached the landing, they called me over to the kitchen table.

"It's time to make a final decision about college," said my dad.

"I'm going to get a job in the funeral industry, the only vocation I consider real," I said.

"Not so fast," said my dad. "We want you to think about this."

"I've thought about it," I said. "I'm not going to college. That's my final decision."

My mom started sobbing. "Your dad and I... think it's best... if you stay home tonight... and really sit with this."

"That's bullshit," I said.

"You're not allowed to leave the house until you make a final final *final* decision," said my dad.

I looked out the kitchen window. Dylan's Buick was in the driveway. He beeped his horn and waved a Ziploc bag full of hairy green orbs. I stood up to go.

My dad grabbed my arm. "Final final final," he said.

"Okay, fine," I said. "I'll go to college."

4

Higher Education

The University of the Pacific Northwest was a fairy tale of brick castles, manicured lawns, and concrete paths that criss-crossed campus with a meandering geometry reserved for the daydreaming progeny of oil tycoons. The students had names like Bunny, Chet, and Blair. They'd spent their summers white-water rafting and backpacking the Pacific Crest Trail. I tried to make friends with them, but I didn't know what a carabiner was. Rapids scared me. I'd spent my summer holed up in the public library, researching *chikhai*, *chonyid*, and *sidpa*, the three bardos described in the *Tibetan Book of the Dead*.

Instead of playing beer pong and having premarital sex, I sat on the concrete steps of my residence hall, chain smoking and reading books that hadn't been assigned for class. Heady tomes by Camus, Salinger, Nietzsche, and Dostoyevsky.

"What book is that?" asked a kid from my History of Western Civilization class who everybody called "Izod," due to his extensive collection of Polo shirts.

"*Crime and Punishment*," I said.

"What's it about?" he asked.

"This guy named Raskolnikov decides to kill an old lady for no reason and then feels bad about it."

"Sick," said Izod, smacking gum. "Know where to get weed?"

I shook my head no.

He covered a nostril and exhaled, launching a hefty snot rocket onto the ground near my feet.

"Good talk," he said and walked away.

These were the people my parents had sent me here to befriend. They drank Milwaukee's Best and wore hemp necklaces and backward baseball hats. Nothing bad had ever happened to them and nothing ever would. They'd join a fraternity, commit light sexual assault, and end up running their father's investment firm one day. A few of them would run for Congress and win.

I put out my cigarette and went inside. My dorm room was half-covered in Claudia Schiffer posters, half in quotes I'd typed out on my Smith Corona typewriter.

The Schiffer half belonged to my roommate Todd. He was lying in bed, absentmindedly turning the pages of a *Hustler* magazine.

"How's it going, Todd?" I asked.

"You know how women have thoughts and feelings?" he said.

"Yeah."

He turned the page to a centerfold featuring an airbrushed woman with fake breasts, casually prying her vagina apart. "It's fucking weird."

I sat on my bed and looked up at the quotes on my wall. There was one from Thoreau's *Walden*: "I went to the woods because I wished to live deliberately… and not, when I came to die, discover that I had not lived."

And one from Henry Miller's *Tropic of Cancer*: "I have no money, no resources, no hopes. I am the happiest man alive."

And another I copied from Louis Fischer's *Gandhi: His Life and Message for the World*: "St. Francis of Assisi was hoeing his garden when someone asked what he would do if he were suddenly to learn that he would die before sunset that very day. 'I would finish hoeing my garden,' he replied."

I stood up and looked out the window. It was a beautiful fall day. Students in polar fleeces sauntered about like the children of Zeus. By their fearless demeanor, you'd think they owned the world. Some of their parents did.

A boy wearing a Beta Theta Pi sweatshirt waved to a girl in Delta Delta Delta sweatpants. She was a skeleton under her breasts and hair. He didn't care. They'd meet up later to drink beer and fornicate with their giddy loins. It was how the commoners avoided Yama, the Lord of Death.

I was about to go outside for another cigarette when I looked into a nearby field and noticed a dozen hippie girls in patterned dresses. Every 30 seconds, one of them squatted, ripped something out of the lawn, and tucked it into a makeshift kangaroo pouch formed by the hem of her dress. A second later, she was upright as if nothing had happened. The collective effect looked like something out of a Eugène Ionesco play.

"Hey, Todd," I said. "Have you noticed the girls in the quad?"

"What girls?" he asked, sitting up.

"They're leaning over and picking things out of the grass."

He joined me at the window. "Oh—*them*. They're harvesting."

"Harvesting what?"

"Blue ringers."

In a chance convergence of drug and test subject, the quad adjacent to our freshman dorm was overrun with *psilocybe stuntzii*, a psychoactive toadstool also known as "Blue Ringers." Every fall, a handful of thrill-seeking freshmen, undaunted by the prospect of losing their shit for four to six hours, drank a magical tea brewed from the wild-harvested fungi.

The idea of cracking open my third eye with a mycological crowbar appealed to me. I'd read *The Teachings of Don Juan*. I knew that cactuses could turn men into shapeshifting wizards, and that our destinies were often foretold by sorcerers masquerading as ravens. Maybe the plant kingdom could teach me a less shitty meaning of life than the one TV and movies had been teaching me for the last 18 years.

I paid a visit to my classmate Claire. She was in her dorm room, standing over a coffee maker, dumping stringy mushrooms into a frilly white filter.

"I heard you have some Blue Ringers," I said.

"A few," she said. "Probably not enough to do anything."

"I don't know. That seems like a lot."

The mound of fungi rose 2 to 3 inches above the top of the filter. There was a plastic Safeway bag full of mushrooms on her bed and another on top of the television.

We put on a Grateful Dead concert video and sat on her couch. The tea tasted like dirt and poison. I didn't like it, but I was determined to get high, so I drank it to the bottom and swished the grit between my teeth. I didn't think it was working, but during the guitar solo in "Sugar Magnolia," I made the startling discovery that the glands in my neck were multidimensional pink geodes. Something went *Zing!* in my mind, and suddenly I was full of energy.

I didn't know what to do with it, so I went outside, took off my clothes, and started running laps around the quad. People gave me high-fives. They thought I was a streaker. They didn't know I was in metaphysical communion with my own wind resistance.

I ran around for nearly an hour before campus security returned the meat-skeleton of my current incarnation to my dorm room. Luckily, the cops were in a fraternity with my brother Pete. They mistook my antics for a hazing ritual, a crime they immediately pardoned. They helped me put on my underwear, wished me luck in Sigma Chi, and said goodnight.

I ate mushrooms five or six more times that fall until my third eye became permanently ajar. I stopped going to class. Instead, I visited philosophy professors during their office hours to ply them with questions about the nature of reality. Their answers were pedantic and simplistic; not one mentioned the Mayan calendar or self-transforming machine elves.

After I'd grilled them for an hour or two, laughing inwardly at their terrestrial responses, they asked me which class of theirs I was in.

I said, "Oh, I'm not in your class."

They said, "Wait. So why are you here?"

I said, "That's what I'm trying to find out!"

I stood up and walked outside—an incredible place a million times better than inside. Trees and plants grew everywhere. Not to mention grass, those miniature green spears yearning for the sun.

I started thinking about clothes. They didn't make any sense. What did Adam and Eve have to do with my beautiful pink body? I took off my pants and underwear and gazed up at the puffy clouds. What beautiful shapes!

When campus security found me this time, they discerned in my serenity not a hazing ritual, but the goggle-eyed wonder of a freshman who'd fried his brain on drugs.

They took me into custody, but they weren't real cops; their only recourse was to make me write a letter to my parents, confessing what I'd done.

I said, "Good idea! It's about time they knew the truth!"

I wrote the following letter, which I discovered in a shoebox my mom returned to me a few years ago when she was cleaning out the attic of my childhood home:

Dear Mom and Dad,

I have eaten medicine sent here by aliens. There are fractal patterns everywhere. Thank you for raising me from a zygote. College is good, but there is too much beauty. It is scary learning everything. My philosophy professors are okay, but my best professors grow in the quad, a place like Eden that inspires me to shed my false garments. Speaking of which, I seem to be under arrest. My captors don't have any power, at least not that they're aware of. They haven't eaten medicine. Have you been outside lately? Plants grow there. They have things to teach us. Lately I'm interested in rhododendrons, but don't forget Douglas firs, the wizards of the Pacific Northwest!

Love,
Kevin

5

Gummy Bear

It was clear I could learn more from a careful reading of *Zen and the Art of Motorcycle Maintenance* than I could from the entire Western educational system, so I dropped out of college, returned to Beaverton, and got a job sorting recycled goods at Wild Harvest, an organic foods grocery store. By day, I stacked apple cider vinegar bottles into geometric towers that resembled visions I'd seen at the peak of my psychedelic experiences. At night, I sat at a Formica table in an apartment I shared with my old friend Dylan, reading about the nature of "quality" while tenderly sipping Robitussin.

I was happier than I'd ever been. In many ways, my life was like the Zen monks of Japan who spend their days chopping wood and carrying water, hoping in this way to achieve the lightning insight of satori.

One afternoon, I was on my lunch break reading *The Electric Kool-Aid Acid Test* when I came upon a passage about a stoned Hells Angel making love to a beautiful hippie woman in a tree. As I read, something stirred in my underwear. It was an erection.

I did some math on the back of a receipt and realized I was 20 years old and still a virgin. I decided that in addition to enlightenment, I should seek out intercourse since it too might have lessons to teach me.

As luck would have it, there was a barista at the coffee shop next to Wild Harvest who I happened to be in love with. Her name was Angela. She was beautiful and insane. She believed the end of the world was imminent, a conviction she'd arrived at while high on LSD. She wore a leather jacket, had an infinity symbol tattooed on her wrist, and didn't shave her armpits.

I decided to ask her on a date.

She said no.

I tried again a few days later, and she said, "Definitely not."

The third time I asked, she said, "My friend Irma and I want to take a date-rape drug with our spiritual advisor, Gummy Bear, but we're afraid he might rape us. We need a lookout. Are you in?"

The idea of going on a date with a woman so she could roofy herself without fear of sexual assault made me uncomfortable, but I said, "Yeah, that sounds awesome."

Gummy Bear looked like the kind of guy who told 19-year-old hippie girls that LSD was all right, but this other stuff, GHB (which just happened to be a date-rape drug), was way cooler. He was in his mid-to-late 50s, drove a VW bus, and wore an electronic ankle monitor that he told us not to worry about.

"Who's this guy?" he asked when we showed up at his apartment.

"This is Kevin," said Angela. "He's in charge of recycling at Wild Harvest. He's cool."

"How do I know he isn't a cop?"

"Just look at him."

I was wearing corduroy pants, Birkenstocks, and a Lollapalooza '93 t-shirt covered in elaborate tribal designs.

Gummy Bear looked annoyed but decided I wasn't a cop.

"So, here's the deal," he said, producing an amber vial. "First, fill up the dropper. Then squeeze it on your tongue. Right away, you'll feel a pleasant head rush. After that, you might need to take a nap for seven or eight hours. Feel free to lie down on my bed. Except you, Kevin. You get the couch."

Angela and Irma nodded excitedly.

Irma went first. She put some GHB on her tongue and let it slide around.

"It tastes like semen," she said and swallowed it.

"Far out," said Gummy Bear.

Angela was next. She took it into her mouth and swirled it around. I thought the plan was for me to stay level-headed and cool to make sure Gummy Bear didn't rape anybody, but suddenly Angela turned to me and, in a spontaneous gesture, kissed me. As she did, she spit the GHB into my mouth. I swallowed it.

An hour later, Irma and Angela were passed out on Gummy Bear's bed.

For some reason, the drug didn't affect me. Compared with all the psilocybin I'd ingested in college, it may as well have been Tylenol.

Gummy Bear and I sat on the couch, watching *Forrest Gump* on VHS.

"Aren't you tired?" he asked.

"I feel great," I said. "Wide awake. Man, I forgot how good this movie is."

"Yeah, it's amazing."

Forrest Gump was in love with his childhood friend Jenny, but she wasn't in love with him because he had developmental disabilities. It was the same as my situation with Angela, except my brain was fine; I was just awkward and nervous all the time and fell in love with girls who roofied themselves for fun.

"Some of this feels far-fetched," I said. "Like, I can see Forrest becoming an international ping pong champion, but the part about him discovering the Watergate break-in? I mean, c'mon."

"I don't know, brother," said Gummy Bear. "I think you just have to go with it."

Gummy Bear kept asking if I wanted to take a nap or get lost for an hour or two, but after a while he gave up. We watched *Apollo 13*, *Big*, and half of *Sleepless in Seattle*.

Eventually Angela stumbled out of the bedroom. She said she wanted to go home. I drove her and Irma back to Irma's apartment and tucked them into bed with their clothes on.

The next day Angela called and said, "Thanks for making sure we didn't get raped! You're the best."

I said, "No problem. It was fun."

After that, Angela and I did pretty much everything together, except make love, since I was the sworn protector of her chastity.

6

Name a City

Five days a week, from 10 a.m. to 4 p.m., I inhabited the dimly
lit back room of Wild Harvest, sorting Blue Sky Soda cans into
colored bins, rinsing plastic yogurt tubs, and compressing zucchini boxes in the cardboard baler. Then my shift ended, and
I walked next door to Angela's coffee shop and sat at an outdoor
table, drinking overpriced lattes while reading treatises on astral
travel.

On Angela's break we smoked and talked about our drug
experiences. I told her about my psychedelic expeditions at the
University of the Pacific Northwest, shedding my pants while
communing with the plant kingdom. She told me about all the
raves she'd attended at the age of 14, high on ecstasy.

During one of these conversations, Angela recounted the trip
that convinced her the end of the world was imminent. She was
at a Rainbow Gathering in Eugene, Oregon. Her dealer, Gummy
Bear's cousin, Lucifer, sold her five tabs of acid, apologizing that
the stuff was kind of bunk and probably wouldn't do anything.

Angela put all five tabs on her tongue.

"No wait," he said. "My bad. That's the new stuff. It's crazy strong."

Angela spit out four tabs, but it was too late—the LSD was already working its way into her bloodstream.

She sat in a field of hippies who she mistook for the monolithic pillars of Stonehenge. The sun slanted and the pillars' shadows told the story of Life and Death. Then a seven-headed dragon appeared and commanded her to gather a team of men and women with specific survival skills like basket making and animal husbandry.

"The End of Days is coming," said the dragon. "You can't rely on civilization to feed and shelter you. Only the capable will survive."

I thought Angela was exaggerating, but a few months later, she said the time had come for her to be tested. She'd signed up to volunteer as a relief worker in Africa, giving vaccines to people in remote villages.

"I'm going to find out if I have what it takes to survive the Apocalypse," she said.

"Right on," I replied, taking a deep drag off my American Spirit cigarette.

"What about you?"

"Africa? No thanks. I'll just stay here and read *The Doors of Perception*. Maybe eat some peyote buttons and figure out once and for all if there's life after death."

"Life's so much bigger than Beaverton, Oregon," said Angela. "Quick—name a city. The first place that comes to mind."

I took a sip of my latte. I didn't want to name a city. Angela was always making me do things I didn't want to do.

"I don't know," I said.

"C'mon. Don't think about it. There's no wrong answer. Just say something."

"San Diego."

"San Diego? Why San Diego?"

"I don't know. It was the first place I thought of."

"Yeah, but like—why not New Orleans?"

"I didn't think of New Orleans. I screwed up."

I tried to change my answer, but Angela said it was too late. My fate had been decided by my unconscious mind. I had to move to San Diego. It was my destiny.

I sold my Fender Stratocaster and my childhood collection of Reggie Jackson baseball cards and bought a bus ticket to San Diego. Angela was wrong. San Diego was amazing. There were palm trees and beaches and surf shops and rooftop bars where tan people sat around all day drinking Coronas. I found a room in a youth hostel for $8 a night and subsisted on fish tacos, which you could buy 2 for $3 at little carts scattered throughout the city.

I only had $100 to my name, but instead of scouring the classified ads for a job, I bought a copy of Joseph Campbell's *The Hero with a Thousand Faces* and sat on the beach all day, reading about fairy tales and vision quests. I was so enthralled that I forgot to get a job and ran out of money.

I called my mom and said, "Mom, I followed the mythical creature into the forest, but in my excitement, I abandoned my journey to read a book about my journey. I won't make the same mistake again if you wire me some money."

She said, "Are you on drugs, Kevin?"

I said, "Not anymore. I'm on a spiritual quest."

She agreed to Western Union me $100 on the condition that if I didn't find a job, I'd come home, cut off my long hair, and go to work for my dad's electrical contracting company.

Instead of reading about the hero's journey to the underworld, I sat on a park bench near the ocean, perusing the classified section of the *San Diego Union-Tribune*. The paper was full of ridiculous occupations like "accountant" and "registered nurse," words I hadn't encountered once in my study of the world's religions.

The only job I was remotely qualified for was "outdoor school instructor." According to the ad, Orange County was looking for Southern California's best and brightest to teach inner city youth about the great outdoors. The job required you to live and work in the San Bernardino Mountains, two hours east of Los Angeles.

I called the 1-800 number.

A woman answered. She said, "Do you like kids?"

I said, "They're great. I'm basically a child myself."

She said, "Do you have a criminal record?"

I said, "Not that I'm aware of."

She said, "You're hired."

7

Googolplex

For the next six months, I made my living singing "Boom Chicka Boom" to a gangly pack of sixth graders so grateful to be outside the drab confines of their classroom that they treated us, their Birkenstock-wearing elders, like gods. We went on nature hikes, whittled snakes from tree branches, and performed skits mocking our camp principal, Margaret Gosselin, who we likened, depending on the fancy of that week's campers, to Adolf Hitler or Darth Vader.

Every Monday, a school bus arrived with a fresh group of campers. All the boys wanted to be in Squirrel's cabin. Squirrel was blond and had nice teeth and projected confidence, whereas I didn't wash my hair and projected anxiety and delusions of grandeur.

While Margaret read the campers' names, they all mouthed the same prayer: *PLEASE SAY SQUIRREL PLEASE SAY SQUIRREL PLEASE SAY SQUIRREL*.

"Carlos Lopez… Squirrel. Javier Hernández… Squirrel."

The boys exchanged high fives and pumped their fists.

My counselor name was "Googolplex." When Margaret assigned an unlucky camper to my cabin, his lower lip quivered, and the other boys taunted him as if he'd soiled his pants.

I led my dejected campers back to our cabin and gave them a pep talk.

"Listen," I said. "I know I wasn't your first choice for a counselor. I wasn't your second or third or fourth choice. I know my voice quivers when I talk. I haven't washed my hair since 1996, but here's the thing. Squirrel has bad farts. One of his campers died last week. From farts. Your friends celebrating out there today… they're in for a week of sulfur-induced nightmares."

My campers looked at each other in awe. In 10 seconds, I'd completely flipped their worlds upside down. They couldn't believe their luck having escaped a week of horrible, stinky farts.

For the rest of the week, whenever we lined up next to Squirrel's cabin, we covered our faces with bandanas and looked at them with pity. Rumors went around. Squirrel's campers started imagining that Squirrel really did fart all the time. Bad ones. Some of his campers defected and tried to join our cabin, but we wouldn't let them. We made them rejoin their stinky king.

I had a hard time making friends with the other counselors. Most of them worked second and third jobs, trying to save up enough money to attend community college, whereas I'd dropped out of an expensive private university that my parents were paying for because I had epistemological differences with my professors, who I accused of maliciously propagating the status quo.

Only one counselor took pity on me. Her name was Sparkle Pony. She was 53 years old, drove a Trans Am, and had a pretty serious methamphetamine problem. Her nature hikes involved a lot of swordplay with tree branches that, on one occasion, resulted in a camper going temporarily blind.

One Friday afternoon, as we were singing our last *"boom chicka boom"* to the departing campers, Sparkle Pony asked if I wanted to catch a ride into town and spend a few hours at the Family Fun Amusement Park. She promised to return me by dusk so I could spend the weekend hiding from civilization. I really wanted to read an essay about a brisk walk Henry David Thoreau took in 1842, but I said okay.

Sparkle Pony piloted her Trans Am down the mountain in a frightening blur. When we reached San Bernardino, she fed me massive rips from a 3-foot bong, and delivered me, stumbling and coughing, to the Fun Park. We rode around on a Ferris wheel that, on closer inspection, turned out to be a merry-go-round, and then we ate cotton candy that disappeared in our mouths, turning into flavorful air, and then Sparkle Pony said, "Hey, let's play laser tag," and suddenly we were suited up in armor covered in red lights that blinked when somebody shot us.

The referee said, "Everybody ready?" on an intercom.

I said, "Wait, I think my gun—"

The music started playing and a small child shot me, and I died. I had to leave the play center for five minutes, and then I was reincarnated and allowed to join again.

The little kids were the worst. They moved like panthers in the night. I was tall, so I kept getting shot in my helmet. There was nowhere to hide. Everybody thought it was funny, but I was afraid for my safety. My heart was beating like the bass drum at a Megadeth concert, and my field of vision kept going *thunk-thunk-thunk* to the left.

While I was distracted by heart palpitations, one of the little brats shot me in the eye. I sank to my knees. My brain felt like a flamingo stretching its wings, and suddenly I recalled a scene from the movie *Amadeus*, which I'd seen as a young boy. It was the finale of Mozart's opera, *Don Giovanni*. A man dressed as a statue with wings on his helmet burst through a wall and sang, *Don Giovanni a cenar teco, m'invitasti e son venuto!* Of course, this was Death, the secret passageway to God.

A few years ago, I read *VALIS* by Philip K. Dick. He too was shot in the eye with a laser beam and saw the face of God. One day it will happen to all of us.

8

Apocalypse Now

When the school year ended, I was out of a job, so I moved back to Beaverton. I didn't know what to do with myself. I'd completed my spiritual quest. I was like a haggard Achaean come home from the Trojan War, only I was wearing a tie-dye t-shirt and a wooden name tag with the word *GOOGOLPLEX* written on it in purple Sharpie. I started feeling depressed. I'd peaked too early. I was like one of those high school jocks who forever reminisces about his glory days, only my glory was being alone in a cabin at 3,000 feet, reading essays about walking.

My dad repeated his offer to get me a job at his electrical contracting company on the condition that I cut my long red hair. Reluctantly, I agreed. My perdition, in the form of gainful employment and health insurance, was inevitable. There was only so long you could earn your living singing *"boom chicka boom"* to a gangly pack of sixth graders. At some point, you had to join the ranks of men like my father and become chronically depressed, earning money all day so you could fail to buy happiness.

I went into the bathroom, took a beautiful lock of hair between my fingers, and opened the metal mouth of the scissors. Just then the phone rang. It was Angela. She asked if I wanted to go to Montana.

I said, "What's in Montana?"

She said, "I don't want to talk about it. Are you in or what?"

I closed my eyes and tried to picture a life with short hair: eating healthy, going to the gym, listening to Dave Matthews Band until I had a nervous breakdown in a Pottery Barn.

I said, "Okay, sure."

I threw a few shirts in a bag, told my mom and dad I was going to Montana, and hopped in Angela's truck.

Angela and I didn't talk on the drive. She rolled cigarettes, and I asked her questions, which she pretended she hadn't heard. She was suffering from PTSD, a result of her botched relief mission in Africa. I only got bits and pieces of the story, but from what I gathered, upon arriving in Angola, Angela took an immediate dislike to the leader of her organization. She accused him of lacking in leadership skills, and he accused her of being a bitch. There was a mutiny, which failed. Fleeing Luanda, Angela was detained at the Angola-Namibia border. There was talk of marrying her off to a village elder. Another member of her group, a Malibu surf instructor named Chip, found her and pretended to be her husband. He bought her freedom with a case of Budweiser and a Zippo cigarette lighter.

We snaked our way up the Columbia River Gorge, spent the night in the onion country of Walla Walla, then began our ascent of the Rocky Mountains. On the outskirts of Bearmouth, Montana, Angela finally broke her silence. Not to tell me where we were going, but to outline her survival strategy for the biblical End of Days.

"Not everybody's going to die," she said, plucking a strand of loose tobacco from her tongue. "A handful will survive. I intend to be one of them. I'm taking a CPR class this fall. Learning kung fu and beekeeping. Money will be obsolete in the new society. We'll be judged by our ability to provide food and shelter to our fellow man."

I checked to see if she was joking, but she was serious. Her eyes were so blue they glowed in the dark. The white moon hung low in the sky like the blazing eye of a deranged god.

"That's the reason I can't have sex with you," she said. "I need a man who knows how to work with leather. Forge tools from wrought iron. Someone who can gut a wild boar if needed."

"I could gut a boar," I said.

Angela ignored me. She lit a fresh cigarette off the flaming orange nub of her previous cigarette and rolled down the window. A powerful scent filled the cab. Twenty years later, I still think about it. Montana smelled like alfalfa and wildflowers crushed inside a blender. Like geology and time and glaciers melting, pushing mountains around like chess pieces. Breathing filled me with desire. I imagined sucking on Angela's small, paranoid breasts. I'd seen them once by accident through the neck of her loose-fitting hippie gown. They scared me. They seemed too good for a world where Bill Clinton was president and *That '70s Show* was the top-rated sitcom on TV.

9

Frontier Village

At midnight we pulled into a parking lot next to a wooden fort surrounded by rough-hewn logs. It looked like something out of Disney's Frontierland, only seedy—Big Thunder Mountain featuring a dopesick Davy Crockett. There was a covered wagon out front next to a Geo Metro, two horses tied to a satellite dish, and a hand-painted sign reading "SALOON" covered in illicit graffiti.

A woman appeared from inside the fort, wearing buckskin pants and a 10-gallon hat. I recognized her. It was Irma, Angela's friend who thought date-rape drugs tasted like semen.

"Well, look who's here," she said. "Welcome to Frontier Village!"

She invited us into her apartment, a cozy room on the second story of the fort.

"How was your drive?" she asked, loading a bong full of marijuana covered in purple hair and sticky crystals.

"Magical," I said.

"Frustrating," said Angela.

We took turns taking hits, and then Irma told us about Frontier Village. It was a roadside attraction, she explained, a place for bored drivers to pull over while *en route* from Great Falls to Pocatello. Once a bustling Wild West amusement park featuring horseback rides, dinner theater, and the chance to have your photograph taken with an 8-foot stuffed grizzly bear named "Old Ben," Frontier Village had fallen on hard times. When the park's founder, Jack "Outlaw" Quinby, died in a stagecoach accident, a German couple, Klaus and Greta Müller, purchased it at auction. They were running it into the ground. The problem was their eenie-meenie-minie-moe approach to U.S. history. Walking around the faux-storefronts and saloons of Frontier Village, it wasn't uncommon to come upon Klaus wearing a bowler hat, World War II bomber jacket, and the bone necklace of a Lakota Indian.

"Velcoom to the Viiuld Viiuld Vest!" he'd say, pretending to shoot his guests with a pair of plastic squirt guns molded to resemble AK-47s.

The tourists didn't know what to make of it. They asked for their money back.

Irma was insane, but in a totally different way than Angela. LSD had convinced her that the earth was a vicious cesspool of back-stabbing sadists intent on destroying her good time. Boyfriends, coworkers, her own mother—pretty much everybody in Irma's worldview was united in a conspiracy against her, trying to drag her down. She referred to the worst of these conspirators as "energy vampires."

Klaus and Greta belonged to this category. They hadn't paid her in weeks. They hadn't paid anybody. The dozen or so hippies who prepared meals, washed dishes, and sold postcards at Frontier Village worked for free on the vague promise that they'd be paid "eventually." Given the hippies' aversion to capitalism, the ruse worked surprisingly well. It was only when everybody ran out of money to buy drugs that the employees threatened to strike.

"They keep saying they'll pay us next month," said Irma, launching a smoke ring off her tongue. "They've been saying that since April. I don't get it, man. Everywhere I go—energy vampires!"

She stuck her hand down her jeans and loudly scratched her pubic hair. Angela sat on Irma's bed, rolling her 40th cigarette in 24 hours. I sat on a beanbag chair, wondering how much longer I could remain on Planet Earth, a 21-year-old virgin surrounded by oversexed witches.

Irma let Angela and I sleep on the floor for two nights, but then she decided we too were energy vampires and told us to get out. I asked Angela what we should do. She said she wasn't interested in exchanging our hard work for vague German promises. Then she lit a cigarette and looked toward the hills as if she were seeking the answer to our problems in the Montana skyline.

She was.

"Up there," she said, pointing toward a gentle slope rising behind Frontier Village. "We'll pitch a tent. Hide out. Klaus and Greta won't even know we're here."

I wasn't a hundred percent sure why we were there in the first place, but sleeping in a tent with Angela rekindled my hope that one day we'd repopulate the post-apocalyptic earth with nervous red-headed babies.

We put our gear in backpacks, hopped a fence, and made our way up the slope. The view from the hilltop was stunning. You could see for a hundred miles in every direction: yellow hills spotted with western larch, the Missouri River carving a crooked path to St. Louis, and in the distance, the sun like a jeweled pizza cutter slicing the sky from the valley.

The only problem was that our campsite appeared to be on private property. Cows roamed freely in our midst.

"Is it okay that we're here?" I asked.

"It's fine," said Angela, staking the tent. "It's part of the earth. Nobody *owns* the earth."

It was my understanding that people did own the earth, that the planet was chopped into a billion little parcels distributed, in this part of the country, primarily to white people of European descent who bore firearms and shot anyone who trespassed on their land. Judging from the bumper stickers I'd seen since arriving in Montana, killing trespassers appeared to be a pastime here, on par with horseshoes and badminton.

"What if the cows attack us?" I asked.

"They're cows. Cows don't attack. You're thinking of bears."

I wasn't thinking of bears. I looked at a cow. Its bulbous black eye was the most terrifying thing I'd ever seen. I imagined a stampede, one of those razor-edged hooves puncturing my skull with the unthinking violence of a hole punch making a circle in paper.

At dusk Angela and I got stoned, checked to make sure the coast was clear, then followed the path up the hill to our camp. Illuminated by flashlight, the inside of our tent looked like a sex grotto. There was a tapestry, incense burning in the corner, and Ravi Shankar playing on a battery-powered boombox. If Angela hadn't stated so explicitly that she wanted nothing to do with my sad pink genital, I would have taken off my pants and prepared to make love.

Angela wanted to read passages from D.H. Lawrence's *The Rainbow* to each other before falling asleep without having sex. I wanted to try six or seven positions from the *Kama Sutra* and spend the rest of the night coming up with baby names inspired by famous French philosophers.

We compromised. Angela read D.H. Lawrence to me in her nightgown while I rested my head on her stomach like a baby. It was the best feeling of my life. As she read, I barely listened. "Harvest," she said. "Clergy. Nottinghamshire." In my imagination, we were living in a cottage in northern England. Angela was grieving the death of our son Benjamin, a victim of the recent typhoid epidemic. I worked in the fields all day, harvesting wheat with my trusted scythe.

Evening came, and I walked through the front door, covered in sweat. My peasant's smock hung open, revealing a pelt of orange chest hair.

"Oh, Kevin," she said. "I miss our little Benjamin."

"We can make another Benjamin," I said, ripping open her bodice.

I threw her onto the bed and penetrated her like a plough burrowing into the earth.

"What do you think so far?" asked Angela.

"It's good," I said. "I like it."

The first two nights we lived in unhealthy matrimony, playacting mother and 6'6" child, but the third night it got cold in the tent. Angela said, "Fuck this," and left me to go sleep in Irma's bed. The fourth night she sent me up the hill alone. She said she'd be up in an hour or two, but she never came.

I was alone in a cow pasture, confused and sexually frustrated, but free in a way I look back on now as one of the happiest times in my life. Night after night, I zipped myself into the sex grotto and tried to figure out what to do with myself. Even though I hadn't listened to the actual words of *The Rainbow*, I'd grown accustomed to our ritual. I tried to keep it up, but now that I paid attention to the plot, the book turned out to be a mind-numbingly dull exploration of class. The sex parts weren't sexy at all; they'd been hallucinations.

I threw the book out the tent flap and dug into my backpack. Before leaving Beaverton, I'd had the good sense to buy a few paperbacks. One was Kurt Vonnegut's *Slaughterhouse-Five*.

For the next three nights, I read that masterpiece by flashlight. Billy Pilgrim traveled to Tralfamadore. He became an optometrist. He hid out in an underground slaughterhouse while the Allied Forces rained 3,900 tons of aluminum shells sloshing with incendiary pellets over the church-spired skies of Dresden.

The sun rose, and I couldn't keep my eyes open. I fell into a deep sleep. In my dreams, I was unstuck in time, just like Billy Pilgrim. One minute I was a baby. The next, I had a beautiful wife and daughter. Then I was back in high school, sitting behind Jessica Nash, watching the gentle undulations of her ponytail. I blinked, and I was 3,000 miles away, a newly divorced dad, sobbing in my car, driving around the Green Mountains of Vermont.

When I woke up at noon, a heifer was pushing her black nose against the tent fabric, making sounds like I imagined dinosaurs made in the Jurassic period—175 million years ago, when ferns were like palm trees, before humans ruined the earth.

10

But Jesus...

One day Angela smoked a nugget of weed covered in orange and purple hairs and had a vision of Jesus Christ. She told me about it in the tent. She'd brought bagels and cream cheese that she'd pilfered from the Frontier Village kitchen.

"Man," she said. "I got really stoned at the party last night."

"There was a party?" I said.

"Didn't I tell you? Shit. Yeah, everybody finally got paid, so we pooled our money and bought a bunch of weed and mushrooms. There was a jug band and a fortune teller and a stripper dressed like a naughty version of Joan of Arc. During the tightrope act, somebody handed me a bong. I took a gigantic rip and Jesus appeared. He said it's my sacred duty to ride a motorcycle from Montana to South America via the Panama Canal. He recommended I bring a companion along… *you*."

I should have been pissed about missing the party, but I couldn't stop smiling. Not just because Jesus knew who I was, but because Angela thought I was capable of joining her on a transcontinental quest and not dying.

I'd never ridden a motorcycle. Ever since I was born, I'd been a strong proponent of skin and unbroken bones and skulls without fracture lines zigzagging everywhere. But the idea of making love to Angela in the hills of Machu Picchu was too much. I said, "Rad. Count me in."

I signed up for a weekend motorcycle class at the local community college. During introductions, we shared our reasons for taking the class. A retired postal worker named Phil said he'd recently lost his wife to cancer. Touring America had been their dream. Now he was doing it alone as a tribute to her memory.

A hospice nurse named Nancy said she grew up riding dirt bikes but had never ridden on the freeway. When her best friend died of a rare heart condition, she decided to cash in her life's savings and buy a Honda Gold Wing. She hoped to ride to the Grand Canyon and gaze down into that beautiful orange pit, a place she'd seen in magazines but never in person.

When it was my turn, I said, "This woman I'm in love with had a vision of Jesus Christ. He says we're supposed to ride motorcycles to South America. I don't know what's going to happen when we get there, but at some point, the world's going to end."

Everyone nodded. This was a surprisingly acceptable answer in this land of wheat and religion.

We didn't ride motorcycles the first day. We talked about safety. The instructor said that unlike a car, if you hit a bird while riding a motorcycle, it will knock you off your bike and throw you to the asphalt, where you'll skid along at 65 miles an hour in a plume of feathers and blood. "That's why leather is so important. Jacket at a minimum, but I recommend pants, gloves, and a good pair of boots."

"A bird?" I said, trying to fathom how a chickadee could wreak such havoc.

"Oh sure," said the instructor. "If you're not wearing a visor, a bee can fly into your eye and blind you. I once had to dig a dead horsefly out of my cheek with a pair of needle-nosed pliers."

I imagined Angela and I pulled over next to a highway in Ecuador, digging bug corpses out of our faces. Suddenly our spirit journey didn't sound very sexy.

"Now," said the instructor, turning on the overhead projector. "Let's have a conversation about gravel. I'm going to show you a picture of my friend Steven. Steven only has one ear. Can anyone guess what happened to the other ear?"

Nobody raised their hand. I had a guess, but I didn't want to say it. I wanted a less dangerous spirit journey. I wanted a girlfriend willing to have sex with me even though I was a coward.

I finished my motorcycle class with the highest grade on the written exam and the lowest grade on the field assessment. I was smart and good at tests, but I didn't know how to ride a motorcycle. The instructor passed me anyway.

"Just promise me you'll stick to parking lots for at least six months," he said.

"Safety's my number one priority," I said, fully intending to leave for South America the following Friday.

I couldn't wait to tell Angela. Here was proof that I had a certain degree of competence. Maybe I couldn't gut a wild boar, but I could fulfill the first prerequisite for joining her on a suicidal mission to turn into armadillo food on the highways of Chihuahua.

But when I showed Angela the "M" endorsement on my shiny new Montana driver's license, she seemed confused.

"Weird," she said. "You actually did that?"

"Wasn't that the plan?" I asked.

"It was just something I said one day. I wish you wouldn't take everything I say so seriously."

She explained that while I was taking motorcycle lessons, she'd befriended a charismatic goat farmer named Jed who lived in a school bus.

"He knows all about animal husbandry. That's going to be a valuable commodity in the new world. We're sort of dating."

I said, "What about our motorcycle trip?"

She said, "Yeah, I don't know. I think we'd both die probably. I talked to my mom on the phone. She said she'd disown me if I bought a motorcycle."

I said, "But Jesus…"

She said, "I was really stoned. I don't think it was Jesus."

Irma decided to move to Bellingham, Washington, a genial village on the Canadian border with a reputation for having very chill vibes and zero energy vampires. Angela was going to move into Jed's school bus and learn how to milk goats in exchange for sex. I decided to move as far away from those lunatics as possible.

Angela drove me to the bus station. On the way, she presented me with a gift: a felt cowboy hat. It seemed the state of Montana was seizing Klaus and Greta's assets, including Frontier Village, due to nonpayment of taxes. Hoping to collect their back pay, the employees led a raid on the Frontier Village store, pilfering $5,000 in Western gear.

"Irma wanted you to have it," said Angela.

"That's sweet," I said, pulling the brim down over my long red hair.

"So, where you headed next?"

"I don't know. I thought maybe I'd go to New England. Is that an actual place?"

Angela said that from a survivalist standpoint, Vermont's preponderance of cows and lesbians would form an ideal structure for a new society based on milk and freedom from the patriarchy.

I didn't have a better idea, so when the lady at the Greyhound window asked for my destination, I said, "Vermont."

PART II

A NEW SOCIETY BASED ON MILK AND FREEDOM FROM THE PATRIARCHY

11

The Semi-Retired Large Animal Veterinarian

What can I say about Burlington, Vermont—that quaint New England city where I spent the majority of my 20s, in whose apartment buildings I nearly lost my virginity, then actually lost my virginity? Walking around that first day, I had the sensation that I'd stumbled into the fever dream of a nostalgic suburban housewife. Everywhere I looked, there were brick buildings and church spires and Baby Boomers taking photographs of brick buildings and church spires. They'd come from places like University Park, Texas; New Albany, Ohio; and Los Altos Hills, California, to indulge masturbatory fantasies of "simpler times" that never existed in reality, whereas I'd come to ride out a non-apocalypse, hoping to convince my non-girlfriend that I had the survival skills necessary to have sex with me.

For the five-month period I was employed as an outdoor school instructor in the San Bernardino Mountains, I'd spent exactly $432... $400 on cigarettes and $32 on a day pass to the Family Fun Center, where I got shot in the eye by a laser and saw the face of God. The remainder got deposited directly into my checking account, which at the end of the school year carried the unthinkably vast sum of $9,387. I figured that money would carry me into retirement, right up to the time of my death, whereupon I'd bequeath the balance to my red-headed offspring. But when I stepped up to the first ATM I saw in Vermont and withdrew $200 to pay for a week in a youth hostel, I was astonished to discover that I only had $44 left in my bank account. It seemed I'd squandered a small fortune in Helena on preparations for Angela's aborted South American vision quest—things like bug repellant and motorcycle lessons and *Lonely Planet* guides to Honduras and Peru.

Instead of reading *The Hero with a Thousand Faces*, I bought a newspaper and checked the classified ads. There weren't any listings for outdoor school instructor, so I checked the "P" section, but nobody wanted to hire a poet. I started feeling depressed, so I went to the co-op and bought a tincture of St. John's wort. Squirting it under my tongue, I noticed a HELP WANTED sign in the window. I filled out an application. Two days later I was typing PLU codes into a cash register, asking Bob Ross clones if they remembered the SKU number for their bag of organic spelt flour.

I got an advance on my paycheck, which I used to pay first and last month's rent on a dilapidated apartment. I used a sleeping bag for bedding and stole a few milk crates from work for furniture. For decoration, I went to the library and photocopied pictures of my literary heroes and thumbtacked them to my wall. By my parents' standards I was living in squalor. I'd never been happier.

I only had to work 16 hours a week to make rent, which left me an inordinate amount of free time. The only problem was I didn't know what to do with it. If there's such a thing as reincarnation, this is my first time being human. Most days I strolled up and down Church Street, pretending to be at ease in my bipedal form. To prove how normal I was, I wore a 10-gallon hat, smoked a corncob pipe, and imitated a 21-year-old semi-retired large animal veterinarian from Montana.

I was on one of these aimless strolls, making my sixth or seventh loop from Ben & Jerry's to the Vermont Maple Syrup Emporium, when I noticed a woman smoking a cigarette on a concrete stoop in front of a clothing store called "Gold Dust." She had a Colette haircut, wore a red sweater with holes in the elbows, and bore an uncanny resemblance to George Washington. I couldn't tell if I was attracted to her.

"Afternoon, ma'am," I said, momentarily removing my cowboy hat. "I'm new in town. What do folks do for fun around here?"

The woman smiled. "Depends. What are you into?"

I spit on the ground in the manner of a ranch doctor who'd plundered his fair share of bull scrotums.

"Most Friday nights I'm roping steers," I said. "Chewing tobacco, watching the sun set over the Rocky Mountains. That kind of thing. But a few months ago, I read this book—" I reached into my pocket and pulled out a tattered copy of *Leaves of Grass*. "It changed me. I decided to hitchhike across America. Sing the body electric. Sound my barbaric yawp over the roofs of the world."

"I prefer Salinger," said the woman, producing a slim paperback from her purse.

It was *Nine Stories*, a fine book. I pretended I'd never read it.

"I guess what I'm asking is—where can a fellow find some whiskey around here?" I pulled out my pipe and lit it with a match.

The woman directed me to a bar across the street.

"By the way, I'm Kevin," I said.

"Wendy," she said.

A real cowboy would have invited her to come with him, but I wasn't a real cowboy. I was a nervous pilgrim on a spiritual quest to lose my virginity. I was waiting for a sign.

"Well," I said, tipping my hat. "See you around."

12

The Lion's Den

Wendy and I had the same days off work. Every Tuesday and Wednesday, we sat at adjacent tables at the local coffeehouse, pretending to read obscure novels by Turgenev and Émile Zola while engaged in a 30-minute game of accidental eye contact and periodic pen borrowing. Eventually one of us moved our things, and then we were immersed in a passionate conversation about literature and astrology.

Wendy was an Aquarius with a Scorpio moon and Sagittarius rising. She loved Plath, Chekhov, and Edna St. Vincent Millay. She thought the Beats were a bunch of blowhards who'd misappropriated Buddhist ideology to justify being assholes. I told her I was a Capricorn with an Aquarius moon and Cancer rising and pretended I wasn't on a spiritual quest stemming from my profound love for the faux-Buddhist blowhards she despised.

One day in October, Wendy surprised me by inviting me over to her apartment to meet her cat Humphrey. Humphrey turned out to be just okay, as far as cats go, but Wendy and I spent the next five hours drinking chianti and talking about our childhoods.

Wendy grew up in a poor neighborhood in Boston during the height of the crack epidemic. She lived with her mom and younger sister in a brownstone that marked the dividing line between two rival gangs. One morning Wendy put on her backpack, stepped outside, and saw yellow crime tape surrounding the park across from her house. One of her classmates had been raped and murdered, her body dumped on the metal merry-go-round.

"Jesus," I said.

"We moved to a better neighborhood when I was 15," she said. "But I'd already seen a lot of shit."

I told Wendy about my childhood in Montana, roping calves, breaking horses, and shooting wolves who threatened the herd.

"This one time I was on a hike near Devil's Ridge when I got bit by a rattlesnake. I had to cut an *X* over the wound with my Swiss Army knife and suck the poison out. I still have a limp."

Wendy said, "Holy shit—really?"

I said, "Actually, I grew up in Beaverton, Oregon. It was safe. The worst thing that ever happened was the time Adam Kim tripped over my Nintendo power cord when I was about to kill Ganon in *The Legend of Zelda*."

It didn't matter that I'd lied to her. In this weird, forgotten corner of America, we were hiding from our pasts, playacting adulthood.

When I wasn't drinking wine at Wendy's apartment, bonding with her and sharing our life stories, I was at the public library, researching how to lose my virginity. I wanted to know how to tell which woman was the right one, which sexual position was best, and whether fornication was a help or hinderance on the pilgrim's journey to God.

One afternoon I was sitting in the religious studies section, transcribing my favorite lines from the *Bhagavad Gita* onto 3" x 5" index cards, when two beautiful women holding clipboards approached me. They said they were raising money to fund a relief mission in Africa, where they hoped to save the world by giving vaccines to people in remote villages.

"We're going to find out if we have what it takes to survive the apocalypse," they said.

The more they talked, the more familiar it sounded.

"Wait a second!" I said. "I know exactly what you're talking about."

I told them my friend Angela went to Angola on a similar expedition that resulted in a failed mutiny and her temporary imprisonment.

Suddenly the women were extremely interested in what I had to say.

"Should we be worried?" they asked.

"You should be fine," I said. "Just make sure to carry a case of Budweiser and a Zippo wherever you go."

The women complained that they were sleeping on the cold concrete floor of a church.

"Our backs hurt and everything smells like frankincense," they said.

I wrote my name and address on a piece of paper and said that if they needed a place to crash, they were welcome to stay with me.

An hour later I was sitting on a tatami mat on the floor of my apartment, making an offering to Lord Krishna, when I heard a knock on the door. It was the women. One of them was holding a bottle of whiskey.

I was annoyed, but then it occurred to me that I was on a pilgrimage to lose my virginity, and these women, with their liquor and vaginas, might be able to help me in my quest.

We sat on the floor of my bedroom and took turns slugging whiskey. The women—Sarah and Yvonne—were best friends from Boulder, Colorado. At a Phish concert a few years earlier, they'd accidentally taken five hits of acid and had a profound vision of the end of the world.

"The time has come for you to be tested," I said.

"Yes!" they agreed.

"The world's so much bigger than Boulder, Colorado."

"Exactly!" they said.

Everything I said made them giddy and amazed. I repeated things Angela had said to me a year earlier, and they thought I was a highly evolved hominid with the power of clairvoyance.

I put on a Nina Simone record, hoping it would give the night a philanthropic group sex vibe, but the song that came on was "To Be Young, Gifted and Black."

I scanned the back of the album, trying to find a song that wasn't about institutionalized racism, but it didn't matter. When I turned around, Sarah and Yvonne were on my mattress, kissing and pouring whiskey into each other's mouths.

I was content to sit back and watch this amazing spectacle, but after a minute they turned to me and said, "What are you waiting for?"

I crawled in bed with them. We kissed in a triangle, sticking our tongues toward a central axis where the tips touched.

I put my left hand down Sarah's pants and my right hand up Yvonne's shirt. Somebody had their hand in my pants, tugging on my wiener.

We got naked, but the girls felt self-conscious and made me turn off the lights. For a panicked moment, standing at the light switch, it occurred to me that I was about to lose my virginity to two women at the same time. I had to pick one to put it in first.

It was too dark to see faces. For the rest of my life, I wouldn't know whether I'd lost my virginity to Sarah or Yvonne. The mystery would plague me until my final days. I pictured Arjuna sitting in a golden chariot with his blue friend, Krishna. This world was full of choices. No matter what you did, the consequences extended infinitely through the rest of your life. It was almost impossible to fathom the extent to which every one of our actions rippled into the cosmos.

In my extreme vexation trying to figure out which girl to put it in, I started shivering and spontaneously ejaculated onto the floor. I took off my sock and wiped it up.

"What's taking so long?" the girls asked. "Come here and put your penis into our vaginas."

It was dark. They didn't see what happened. I got back in bed with them. There was a lot of groping, but I couldn't get it up.

"What's wrong with your wiener?" asked Sarah. "Why's it floppy?"

"I can get it hard again," I said. "Give me a second."

I started tugging on it. The women took turns tugging it and kissing it, but it only got smaller, until it shrunk back into my testicles and disappeared completely.

I said, "I don't understand what's happening."

Sarah said, "I have to go to the bathroom."

Yvonne turned on the light.

I kept tugging, hurting myself.

"Wait!" I said. "It's starting to get big again. Quick, open your legs."

"I don't know," said Yvonne. "I'm feeling sleepy."

Sarah came back from the bathroom. She was wearing a bra and panties. Yvonne put a sweatshirt on. The mood was gone. I'd screwed up.

We fell asleep in a pile of underutilized flesh. When I woke up the next morning, they were gone. I felt like I'd spent the night in the lion's den, covered in steaks, and emerged with-out a scratch. It didn't make sense. My virginity was a vagina-repelling force field.

I came to a decision: if I didn't have sex by my 22nd birthday, I'd have my penis and testicles surgically removed so I could enjoy the beauty of the sky and trees and rivers without hating myself because of my inability to find a woman to have sex with because I spent my Friday and Saturday nights reading the *Bhagavad Gita* at the public library.

13

Chronic Tonsillitis

It was December 14, ten days before my penis amputation. Burlington was covered in a foot of snow. Afraid to appear in public as anything less than a hundred percent cowboy, I continued sporting only a frayed pair of vintage leather boots as footwear. Shuffling down Church Street, my toes turned blue as the god I secretly prayed to every night, begging him to use one of his dozen arms to send me a girlfriend.

I had the day off work and ran into Wendy. She asked how I was doing.

I said, "Pretty good, except I totally screwed up this ménage à trois the other night."

She said, "Oh, man. That sucks. Do you want to pick up a bottle of wine, go back to my place, and talk about it?"

An hour later we were sitting on the floor of her apartment, listening to Paul Simon's "Hearts and Bones." We talked about moon signs and T.S. Eliot. Our teeth turned purple. It wasn't even noon.

At one point, Wendy said, "There's something I want to read you."

She reached over to her bookshelf and pulled out a book. It was *Delta of Venus* by Anaïs Nin.

I'd been down this road before. I stretched out on the floor and rested my head on Wendy's lap like a baby.

"What are you doing?" she asked.

"I'm resting my head on your lap like a baby," I said.

"Stop that. It's weird."

I sat up, and Wendy read to me. *Delta of Venus* was the opposite of *The Rainbow*. The sex parts weren't hallucinations. They were pornographically descriptive.

"Her sex was like a giant hothouse flower," read Wendy. "Larger than any the Baron had seen, and the hair around it abundant and curled, glossy black."

Wendy was wearing the same thing as the day we met—a bright red sweater with holes in the elbows. I wanted to reach out and pinch the dry patch of elbow skin through her ragged woolen windows. Instead, we started kissing.

It was a hundred degrees in the room. I put my hands under her sweater. You could've boiled lobsters under there. Paul Simon sang about the Blood of Christ Mountains. I found the clasp of Wendy's bra.

Wendy had a magnificent untrimmed bush. Her vulva looked like a red crayon melted on a fur coat. It scared me. Looking at it, I started to lose my mind. I put a condom on, leaned forward, and blacked out.

When I regained consciousness, I was lying on my back, covered in sweat.

"Did it happen?" I asked.

"What do you mean?" asked Wendy.

"Did we have sex?"

"Ha, yeah. Why?"

"Never mind," I said. "Just kidding."

Wendy and I had sex 20 or 30 times, and then I developed chronic tonsillitis from smoking 20-plus cigarettes a day, outside, in subarctic temperatures. I called my parents to find out if I had health insurance. It turned out I did. While I'd been gallivanting across America, leading nature hikes and sleeping in cow pastures, my dad had been going to work every day, making payments on the house, and providing health insurance to his long-haired prodigal son.

I went to urgent care and asked what was wrong with me.

The doctor looked down my throat and made a disgusted face.

"You don't smoke, do you?" he asked.

"A little," I lied.

"Okay, wow."

"What?" I asked.

"Well—in a healthy individual, tonsils are soft masses of lymphatic tissue that help the body fight off foreign pathogens. Yours are stinky Hot Pockets full of pus and bacteria."

The doctor recommended immediate surgery. When I told my parents, they suggested I fly home to Oregon for the operation so I could recover in a temperate climate that didn't try to kill me every time I walked out the door.

It happened quickly. I remember the airplane landing and the doctor looking into my mouth, saying, "Yeah, let's get rid of those stupid things."

Then I was lying on a gurney under a bright light. The surgeon said, "Count down from 10."

I opened my mouth to say, "Ten," and accidentally swallowed a mouthful of darkness.

When I woke up, I was in the guest bedroom in my parents' house, high on Percocet. My head felt like a helium balloon. If I didn't concentrate on my surroundings, it floated up to the ceiling, and I had to yank the string to pull it back down.

I tried to distract myself with television, but when I clicked the button on the remote control, my face fell off. I looked around for my face and found it on the TV screen, only Billy Crystal was wearing it.

I didn't understand. I seemed to be in a movie. Meg Ryan and I were in love, but we couldn't get along. We kept screwing up our relationship in funny ways that made everyone in the world laugh.

The movie kept going and going. It was amazing. Not amazing, important. I remember thinking, "Has Dostoyevsky seen this?"

When the movie ended, I was pretty sure I'd gone insane.

There was a knock on my door. It was my mom. She said I had a phone call.

I picked up the receiver. It was silent. I waited and waited, but nothing happened.

After a while I heard breathing. I couldn't understand what it meant.

Then I realized I hadn't said hello.

"Hello," I said.

"Hey, this is Wendy! How'd your surgery go?"

I listened but nothing happened. It was a prank call. I'd done the same thing when I was a teenager, calling numbers at random, listening to strangers speak into the void, their peaceful nights ruined by the silence of what they must've presumed was a serial killer.

"Kevin?" said my tormentor.

That name! It used to be mine! What a funny time. I was over it.

I hung up the phone and stared at the ceiling. The popcorn spackle laughed at me. My head started floating. I yanked the cord, and then my mom who gave birth to me in 1976 brought me a cherry-flavored popsicle.

14

The Lizard King

When my tonsils healed, my parents made me a deal. They said they'd buy me a roundtrip ticket to Paris and give me spending money so I could traipse around Europe like a wealthy hobo as long as I promised to come home afterward, choose a career, and spend the rest of my life driving back and forth to work every day, suffering and hating myself.

I didn't want a career, but I wanted to see Jim Morrison's grave, so I said okay. I flew to Vermont, donated all my possessions to the Salvation Army, had sex with Wendy one more time, and flew to Paris.

Europe was fun. People said things I didn't understand, and I replied, *"Je ne comprends pas. Je suis un stupide Américain."*

Here's a complete list of the French words and phrases I learned before traveling to Paris:

1. *Je voudrais un paquet de Gauloises Bleu, s'il vous plaît.*
   "I'd like a pack of Gauloises cigarettes, please."
2. *Où sont les fromages et les baguettes?*
   "Where are the cheeses and baguettes?"

3. *Je ne comprends pas. Je suis un stupide Américain.*
   "I don't understand. I'm a stupid American."
4. *Le Roi Lézard décéda dans ta ville. Ils ont trouvé son corps dans une baignoire. Pouvez-vous me diriger vers sa belle tombe?*
   "The Lizard King died in your city. They found his body in a bathtub. Can you direct me to his beautiful grave?"

I ate baguettes and went to the Louvre and stood under the Eiffel Tower and eventually found Jim Morrison's grave. I took photos with a disposable camera and imagined I was heir apparent to the Lizard King, the great-grandson of Arthur Rimbaud. When I got tired of the city, I took a train to the South of France and found the cobblestone street where Vincent Van Gogh painted *Café Terrace at Night*. The sun set, and I sat on the balcony of a youth hostel in Arles, watching rats scamper across the metal rooftops, imagining all the things I was going to do with my life that had nothing to do with Wendy.

The whole time, she was writing me letters. She sent them to the rank hotel where I was going to spend my final days in Paris. When I arrived, the Frenchwoman at the desk said, "Many mail for you. Very popular. Like celebrity. Here."

I brought the letters to a sidewalk cafe and read them all at once. I still have them hidden away inside a tattered copy of Céline's *Journey to the End of the Night*.

Here's one dated April 17, 1999:

Kevin,

It's Saturday night. I'm sitting on the floor of my bedroom listening to Joni Mitchell's Blue. Do you know the album? It's what I listen to when I feel shaky and alive. Today the sun came out. It was cold, but the air smelled different. I walked around

Burlington inspecting the trees. Report: there are pink blossoms in the cherries, and a white variety whose flowers smell strongly of bleach. I asked a botanist friend. He says this is the Bradford Pear, also known as the "semen" or "spunk" tree. Gross. Sorry about the weird handwriting. Humphrey keeps pushing his face into my hand. He misses you. How do I know this? Because he's being extra annoying. Also, because he sleeps on the Red Hot Chili Peppers shirt you left here. P.S. you left your Red Hot Chili Peppers shirt here. P.P.S. I can't believe I'm dating a man who owns a Red Hot Chili Peppers shirt. P.P.P.S. If you are having sex with some French girl, that's fine. I'm having sex with lots of boys. All with giant cocks. As big as my arm. P.P.P.P.S. Just kidding. I know you're not having sex with a French girl because I'm a witch and I cast a spell on you. Don't believe me? Smell your armpits. Who do you smell? ME. P.P.P.P.P.S. I have an idea. Let's buy a farm and raise goats because the world is stupid, but we are not. 10 goats, 3 chickens, a tomato patch. Bees? When I was a kid, I went to the gardening store with my mom. We bought a bag of ladybugs. They come in a black mesh bag. Would it be unethical of me to buy ladybugs and let them loose in my apartment? Y/N. (Sort of serious about this. Please respond). P.P.P.P.P.P.S. Including a copy of Blue. Going to cost a fortune in shipping but fuck a duck.

XOXO Wendy

Instead of gazing at Toulouse-Lautrec's half-naked dancers or perusing the bookshelves at Shakespeare & Co. on the Seine, I went to a drug store and bought a Sony Walkman and walked down cobblestone alleyways where old men smoked and played chess and housewives hung laundry to dry above iron balconies, the whole time listening to Joni Mitchell sing about sunset pigs and the magical sunshine of California.

15

Rooftop Photography

My return flight to Boston didn't land until after midnight. I wasn't the type of person to arrange for someone to pick me up or have enough money for a hotel. I figured I'd sleep on a bench until the sun rose, then set out on a spiritual journey to find food, shelter, and transportation.

But when I stepped off the plane, I noticed a woman with auburn hair and freckles holding a sign that said, "SEXY REDHEAD."

It was Wendy.

I said, "Holy shit, what are you doing here?"

She said, "Follow me."

We got on the subway and took the silver line to the red line to the orange line and walked up three flights of stairs and entered a one-bedroom apartment with tapestries on the walls and a Gauguin print in the kitchen, depicting a jaundiced Christ with milkmaids praying in the vicinity of his nail-pierced feet.

I said, "Where are we?"

She said, "My friend Stephanie lives here. She's out of town. We can do whatever we want."

I said, "Ooh la la."

Wendy unbuckled my belt and pushed me onto Stephanie's bed and put me inside of her. The sex was so intense, our bodies so young and unguarded, that we both started crying.

Afterward, we wrapped our naked bodies in a blanket and tiptoed up to the roof of the apartment building. The Boston skyline lay before us like a weird dream that a million people were all having at the same time.

Wendy was on her period. Our stomachs were splotched with blood. The blood was alternately bright red and dark red. The dark red was the lining of her uterus. We smelled like a pile of metal shavings after a construction worker cuts a steel stud in half with a Sawzall.

I started blinking.

Wendy said, "Are you okay?"

I said, "Yeah, why?"

She said, "What are you doing with your eyes?"

I said, "I'm taking pictures in my mind. I don't want to forget this."

She thought I was joking, but I was serious. I wanted to remember. I was happy. I couldn't remember having ever been this happy before.

I took as many pictures as I could. I can still see them 20 years later: the glowing windows of skyscrapers, Wendy with her boobs hanging out, and our bellies splattered with blood like we'd just butchered a pig together.

Wendy shivered inside the blankets. We went back inside and had sex again, only slower this time because I didn't have to come. The whole time we looked at each other, trying to fathom what was happening between us, and neither of us knew, and to this day I still don't understand.

Wendy asked if I wanted to visit her mom in Newburyport, a quaint city on the north shore of Massachusetts. I didn't have a job or any responsibilities or plans for the future, so I said sure. We hopped on the train and an hour later found ourselves standing in front of a brick tenement marked by an American flag and a bronze sign that read: James Steam Mill, 1845.

Marion greeted us with a friendly hug and a lit cigarette. She was the opposite of my mom. She swore a lot and listened to the Pixies and spoke incessantly about her spiritual guru, B.K.S. Iyengar, a crackpot yogi whose photograph hung prominently over the fireplace. We sat at the kitchen table, chain-smoking, while Marion told embarrassing stories about Wendy from her childhood.

"Peg was an angel," said Marion, taking a pull off her Virginia Slim. "That's Wendy's sister. She did her homework early, got good grades, and volunteered at the homeless shelter. Not Wendy. All she cared about was boys. There was a line around the block. She was a little slut."

"I was not!" said Wendy.

"You think I didn't notice, but I saw everything. I was just too tired to do anything about it."

After an awkward silence, Marion turned to me and asked, "Do you work out? How's your core?"

I said, "I don't know what that is."

She said, "You have blue circles under your eyes."

I said, "I've had those since the day I was born."

She said, "How are your Kegels?"

I said, "My what?"

Wendy said, "Mom, please don't do this."

Marion went into the other room and came back with a yoga mat.

"Mom," said Wendy.

"I'm just going to show him one position. If you're going to date my daughter, I want to know you have the vitality to give her a proper orgasm."

She started in downward dog, then transitioned into something called the "cobra pose," sticking out her tongue as far as it would go.

"This is a very powerful position," she said, only with her tongue still sticking out, it sounded like, "With ith a wary wow-erwul wowithin."

She made me try. Reluctantly, I lowered myself onto the mat and stuck out my tongue.

"No no no," said Marion. "Really stick it out. All the way. Like this."

I thought Wendy would come to my defense, but for the first time since arriving at her mom's apartment, she seemed to be enjoying herself.

Marion adjusted my hips and told me to concentrate on my "pelvic floor." She kept making small adjustments until, finally, she gave up, saying, "Let's hope for Wendy's sake you have a good sense of humor."

It was unseasonably hot, so we drove to the beach. Wendy wore a striped bikini that showed off her collarbone freckles and belly button ring. We danced in the waves, splashing each other. After a while I got cold and wrapped myself in a towel, but Wendy kept hurling her body over and over into the waves.

Marion sat on a tapestry in a wide-brimmed hat and sunglasses, reading a yoga book. I sat down next to her. I didn't want to talk about my pelvic floor, so I asked her about the only thing we had in common: her daughter.

Marion said Wendy had always been this way. Every time they went to the beach, she had to forcibly drag her daughter out of the ocean. Something about the ocean's vastness and kelp-smell intoxicated her.

I tried to imagine Wendy as someone other than the woman I was making love to. A child: petulant, quick to anger, her freckled face buried in books too adult for her age.

When Wendy bounced back to me, she was shivering. Her fingertips had shriveled up; her thumbs were topographical maps. She wrapped herself in a towel, but she couldn't stop shaking. Her lips were blue. She looked as happy as I'd ever seen her.

Later we were in her childhood bedroom. Our bodies were hot with sunburns. She peeled off her bikini, revealing a bikini of unburned skin. We started kissing. I pressed my fingers into her sunburn; her skin turned white, then red again. Every time we moved, sand poured out of our crevices.

Making love was new to me in 1999. I wore a condom, but it felt like reaching through the lining of Wendy's uterus, rummaging through her small intestine. I knew too much all at once. Too many of my dreams came true. It was too vulnerable, like having your arm broken while simultaneously giving birth.

Afterward we lay in bed, staring at the ceiling, dazed from gazing at bright sand all day. My penis was shiny and damp like a newborn puppy.

Wendy put on Neil Young's *Decade*. While Neil sang and blew his harmonica, I shivered and sprouted goose bumps.

We lit cigarettes. The smoke curled away from us. Wendy told me about the men she made love to when she was still a teenager. Grown men. Friends' uncles. Boys her own age who snuck in through her window back when her mother was exhausted and never woke up no matter how loud her daughter moaned.

Her stories were vivid. Too vivid. I felt like I was sitting on the end of the bed, watching her make love to those other men.

I didn't want to watch. I didn't have any stories of my own. Wendy was my only story.

Wendy revealed something from her childhood too personal to share in this book. Then she said, "Can I ask you a question?"

I said, "Yeah. What's up?"

She said, "I don't want to pressure you or anything, but are we—I mean, am I…" She lifted my hand and laced her fingers between my fingers. For a second, our hands made a fat pink butterfly.

I said, "Are you what?"

She said, "Am I your girlfriend?"

I said, "Oh. Well, I like having sex with you. You're nice."

"*Nice*," said Wendy, nodding.

That wasn't the right answer. She stood up and put her clothes back on, even though I wasn't done staring at her naked body.

Since reading *On the Road* for the first time my sophomore year of high school, and "Howl" by Allen Ginsberg a year later, I thought the purpose of life was zigzagging back and forth across the country, *burning for the ancient heavenly connection to the starry dynamo in the machinery of night*. I decided it was time to hit the road.

Wendy pulled on a pair of boots. "What's your plan?"

"I figured I'd hitchhike to Alaska and ship out on a fishing boat. Either that or work on a farm and milk goats and learn the secret of growing mind-boggling heirloom tomatoes."

"Cool," said Wendy.

I lay there, naked, absentmindedly touching myself.

Wendy said, "Would you mind putting clothes on?"

I said, "I like being naked in your bed."

She said, "You're not very smart."

She lit a cigarette and went downstairs.

16

The Lettuce Farmer

When I got back to Portland, my parents reminded me of our deal. Now that they'd funded my trip to Europe, it was up to me to get serious about life, settle down, and pick a career.

I said, "On the bus, I met this guy named Switchblade. I told him I was trying to decide whether to become a farmer or a commercial fisherman. He said commercial fishing is really dangerous. He recommended farming. I pick farming."

My dad said, "Farming isn't a career."

I said, "Where do you think lettuce comes from?"

He said, "You're going to raise a family growing lettuce?"

I said, "I intend to avoid the trappings of capitalism so I can zigzag back and forth across America *burning for the ancient heavenly connection to the starry dynamo in the machinery of night.*"

He said, "Machinery of what?"

I said, "I'm going to grow vegetables whether you like it or not. It's my destiny."

He called me an ungrateful shit and told me to get out of his house.

I took the bus to the library and did an internet search for "farm jobs." Most of the results were for "agricultural sales" and "equipment operators," but then I came across a listing for an apprentice at an organic farm in Yolanda, Oregon, a small town about an hour south of Eugene.

I borrowed my mom's Cadillac and drove down for an interview. I wanted to make a good impression, so I wore a dress shirt and slacks and one of my dad's ties.

The farmer's name was Arlo. He took one look at me and said, "You know this is a farm, right? I'm not hiring you to do my taxes."

I said, "I wanted to impress you."

He handed me a shovel and said, "Impress me by digging up these garlic bulbs. I'll be back in four hours. If you still want the job after digging for four hours, it's yours. There's a hose if you get thirsty."

The sun was vicious. I'd only been digging for five minutes when I felt a river of sweat dripping from my chin and elbows. I took off my dress shirt and turned it into a turban and harvested garlic bare-chested in my Dockers and Top-Siders.

After four hours, Arlo pulled up on a tractor. "Well?"

"I still want the job," I said. "But I have to return my mom's Cadillac."

"Start Monday?"

"Sounds good."

There are moments in life when you wake up at 6 a.m. and everything hurts because you dig up root vegetables for a living and you're only making a hundred dollars a week and it occurs to you that this isn't so much an "apprenticeship" as an exploitation racket run by opportunistic hippies, but two decades later, when you're sitting at a computer, adjusting the target demographic of a Facebook ad for a health care organization promoting Colorectal Cancer Awareness Month, you look back and realize that being exploited was the best thing that ever happened to you.

I arrived at work Monday in a pair of shiny blue overalls. Arlo put me to work. He showed me how to drive a tractor and water tomato starts and harvest zucchini.

"If you miss one—" he said, gesturing toward a spiny green plant, "—by tomorrow it'll be too big to sell. A zucchini should be 6 inches. If it's any bigger than your pecker, nobody'll buy it."

Arlo drove off, leaving me alone on the farm. He had a real job in Eugene, working as an insurance adjuster. Farming was his side gig—a hobby to keep him from having a nervous breakdown while he was stuck in an office eight hours a day.

I spent the rest of the afternoon watering tomatoes, harvesting lettuce, and yanking garlic out of the ground. At dusk, I closed the gates and sat on the steps of my trailer. Deer grazed on the compost heaps. The sun set orange over the hills. I lit a cigarette and felt the tingle of nicotine deep in my lungs, and for a few minutes I was the happiest man alive. But then stars filled the sky—more than I'd ever seen in my life. The Milky Way revealed itself in the form of a purple arm reaching across the valley, and a meteor shower commenced, launching phosphorus torches from one side of the universe to the other. A pack of wild dogs howled in the hills. It was too much. I couldn't keep that much beauty to myself.

I picked up the phone and called Wendy. It was midnight on the East Coast, but she answered. I told her about Arlo and the meteor shower and the wild dogs. She told me about meeting Stephen King at the inn where she worked.

We talked until four in the morning. I was useless at work the next day, but as I drove the tractor over the hard earth, sending a pillar of dust a hundred feet into the sky, I couldn't stop smiling.

On a scorching afternoon in August, I was picking blueberries and listening to John Coltrane's *A Love Supreme* on my Sony Walkman when Arlo pulled up on his tractor and said I had a phone call. It was Angela. She was back in Portland and wanted to drive down for a visit.

"What happened to Jed?" I asked.

"He was bad at cunnilingus," she said. "And animal husbandry. Most of his goats were sick. I don't think he has what it takes to survive the apocalypse."

I hung up the phone and looked at my arms. They had muscles on them. Real ones that bulged when I flexed. I knew things too—like planting schedules and crop rotation and how to change the blade on a rototiller. I'd never killed a boar, but once, Goldie, the farm dog, bit the wing off a wild turkey and I'd mercifully ended its life with the serrated blade of my Leatherman. This was the closest I'd come to having the survival skills necessary for Angela to have sex with me.

She showed up a few days later in her pickup truck. There was nothing to do on the farm, so we drove to a river and went skinny-dipping.

I couldn't believe it. I'd trembled for weeks the one time I caught an accidental glimpse of Angela's nipple through the neck of her loose-fitting hippie gown, and here she was, naked as Eve.

"Since when do you have muscles?" she asked.

"I've done a lot of digging since the last time you saw me," I said.

"Have you had sex yet?"

"I blacked out the first time, but the second time was amazing."

We swam until sunset, then returned to my shack and lay in bed. I leaned in for a kiss, and Angela said, "Wait a second. I'll be right back."

She disappeared into the bathroom and emerged wearing a nightgown—the same one she'd worn in the love grotto back in Montana. Whatever store she'd bought it from was the opposite of Victoria's Secret. She looked like Sophia from *The Golden Girls*.

She reached into her bag and pulled out D.H. Lawrence's *The Rainbow*.

"We never finished this," she said.

She started reading. I put my head on her stomach. It wasn't the best feeling of my life.

I thought about Wendy 3,000 miles away with her Colette haircut, Anaïs Nin passages, and the red splotches on her body after we made love. I missed her.

17

The Only Thing That Matters

Wendy and I talked on the phone every night until the wee hours of dawn, until it became clear that one of us was going to have to move. I tried to sell her on the merits of farm life, explaining that you only had to work 60 to 70 hours a week in exchange for $100 cash, lodging in a dilapidated trailer, and a terrible rash from rubbing your arms against spiky zucchini plants all day.

Wendy said, "I have a better idea. Why don't you move back to Burlington and move in with me and have sex with me whenever you want?"

Just like that, my agrarian dreams vanished. I wasn't a transcendentalist; I was a dirty dog.

I told Arlo I was leaving the farm so I could explore certain unresolved feelings I harbored for a 22-year-old innkeeper assistant in Northern Vermont.

He said, "Be careful. This is how it starts."

I said, "This is how what starts?"

He said, "The erosion of idealism."

I said, "I just want to make love to my pretty girlfriend."

He said, "That is literally the foundation of capitalism."

I called Wendy and told her I'd be there in about a week and bought a bus ticket to Vermont.

For the third time in less than a year, I was looking out the window as America whizzed by—fields, silos, cows, factories. I wondered about the people who lived and worked in these small towns. Here and there I saw them: talking outside a hardware store, leaning over the hood of somebody's Chevy. Kerouac was wrong. The country wasn't populated by beatniks and angelic hobos. Just men and women waking up at 6 a.m., getting dressed for work, driving their kids to school.

The bus pulled into Burlington at 7 a.m. I hoisted my backpack and hoofed it across town straight for Wendy's. She wasn't expecting me until evening. When I rang the doorbell, she'd just stepped out of the shower. I followed her to her bedroom and watched as she tried to get dressed. She rubbed essential oil into her armpits and plopped on the bed in a red towel.

"It's not fair," she said. "I wanted to surprise you."

She asked me to help fasten her bra. Instead, I took it off and cupped my hands over her small breasts. The heat radiating from her damp skin made her feel like a new thing, just created.

I've slept with 12 women since Wendy. Often the sex is better; I'm more confident, less preoccupied by the fear of ejaculating every second. I slow down, take my time. But I'm not destroyed by the overwhelming intimacy.

With Wendy, it always felt like we were dangling off the edge of a cliff. Afterward we became newborn animals covered in the mucus of birth. I couldn't stop kissing her. I didn't care if I seemed needy or weird. My actions had nothing to do with composure. I was in love. I thought that was the only thing that mattered.

I got my old job at the co-op back, and Wendy and I picked up our relationship where we'd left it like nothing had happened. We hardly worked. Fifteen hours a week was more than enough to pay the bills and still have enough left over for a box of wine and a dozen used CDs. The rest of the time we hung out at Wendy's apartment, having sex. Three, sometimes four times a day until I couldn't come and she couldn't come and I was just moving around inside her and we laughed and Humphrey watched from the windowsill, disgusted. If we fought, it was only about what music to listen to. We each wanted dictatorial control over the record player so we could play our favorite songs for each other, hoping in this way to merge our identities through a shared sense of amazingness.

It was a competition: John Coltrane's "Naima" vs. John Lennon's "Mother." Neil Young's "Sugar Mountain" vs. Nick Drake's "Pink Moon." Bob Dylan's "Oh, Sister" vs. Nina Simone's "Ne Me Quitte Pas."

It wasn't enough that a song was good; the lyrics were a language we were speaking to each other, orienting ourselves in the cosmos of love. Lying on our backs, naked, our genitals shiny and engorged, we listened to Joy Division's "Love Will Tear Us Apart" and spoke in earnest voices about how our love was different than the love of all the couples who came before us.

In particular, our parents. Wendy's were divorced. Mine, I was almost certain, hadn't had sex since March 1976, nine months before I was born.

"I'm not interested in being in one of those marriages where the couple silently hates each other every second of their lives," said Wendy. "I'd rather be a nun. I might be a nun anyway. Just me and Humphrey and a gold cross and my sexy husband Jesus."

"Please don't be a nun," I said.

"I'm serious. I'm not going to be in a loveless marriage. It's not interesting to me at all."

"Me neither," I said.

"Good," she said.

"Good."

As if it was just a matter of saying it out loud. Like our parents hadn't said the same thing, planning their futures together, trying to inoculate themselves against resentment and infidelity.

18

Restless Legs Syndrome

For the first time in my life, I felt settled. I'd logged 23,000 miles on my spiritual journey. I was tired and looking forward to residing in a single location for a year or two, but Wendy had restless legs syndrome, only with her entire body. Less than a month after I'd moved into Wendy's apartment, she said, "Ugh. I'm bored. Let's move to Portland."

Ever since we met, I'd been bragging about my hometown, saying how cool it was because I'd seen a few good shows there in the mid-1990s. Minimizing how lackluster my teenage years had been, I'd inadvertently given her the impression that Portland was the modern-day equivalent of Hemingway's Paris or Ferlinghetti's San Francisco. I'd never intended on going back. But Wendy kept talking about it until I found myself talking about it too, and then we were making plans based on a decision I couldn't pinpoint having ever made.

We sold all our possessions and threw a going away party. I had to work the closing shift. At the end of the night my till was off and the night manager made me stay late. At 11 o'clock

I bolted out of there, afraid I'd missed my own going away party. When I got home, our tiny apartment was crammed with people. There was a DJ in the foyer, dancers in the living room, and friends mulling about the kitchen, engaged in spirited conversation. Everyone assured me the party was just getting started, but I couldn't shake the feeling that I wasn't as buzzed as everybody else, and that if I didn't catch up, they'd realize I was a pathetic loser, unworthy of their friendship.

I cracked open a beer and pounded it and poured myself a glass of wine and guzzled it and loaded a shot of whiskey and took it in one heroic gulp. For a minute, I felt glorious. So glorious I poured myself two more shots of whiskey to celebrate how good I felt.

Then something went wrong in my brain. I remember telling the same story over and over—something about a squirrel I'd come upon that I'd tried to communicate with using a rudimentary language of chirps and buzzing sounds. Then I remember saying, "Oh hey, there's a wall!" Then the world started spinning to the left and the only way I knew how to stop it was to lie down in bed for what I thought would be just a minute or two.

In the morning, I threw up seven times and stumbled into the kitchen. There were people sleeping everywhere.

On the wall, I noticed some kind of chart. Everyone's name was on it who'd been at the party. There were lines drawn between the names.

Wendy walked into the kitchen, holding her head. She sat down, grabbed a waste basket, threw up, and asked if I would make coffee.

"What's this?" I asked, pointing at the chart.

"That's everybody who was here last night. We wrote our names on a sheet of paper and drew lines to connect the people who've slept together."

I looked at the diagram. There were a lot of lines. I had no idea people had so much sex.

I hunted around until I found Wendy. Her name was at the center of the web. There were lines everywhere, shooting in every direction from her name like a thousand-armed god.

It made me sad. Suddenly I didn't feel very special.

"I wish there weren't so many lines," I said.

"I went through a phase before you moved here where I had sex with everybody," said Wendy.

"Oh."

"I told you that."

"I think I just blocked it out."

A guy rolled around on the floor and begged for water. It was one of my coworkers, Jim Foster. I looked at the diagram and found his name. There was a line connecting him and Wendy.

I said, "You had sex with Jim?"

She said, "It was really cold last winter. Jim has a high body temperature."

I decided to let Jim die of thirst.

I went outside and lit a cigarette and looked up into a tree and saw an elegant blue jay preening itself on one of its limbs. I wasn't made for this world. I wanted things to be mine, but they kept belonging to everybody. You couldn't have one single person all to yourself. You had to share. I started coughing and threw up a little, and then I went back inside and gave Wendy a kiss, and the next day we moved to Oregon.

19

Hansel & Gretel

We didn't have enough money for first and last months' rent and security deposit, so we moved into the guest bedroom of my parents' house, which doubled as a doily-infested showroom for my mom's first edition American Girl doll collection. Under the glassy eyes of Samantha, Molly, Kirsten, and Felicity, Wendy and I lay next to each other, not making love.

"We really need to get an apartment," I said.

"I thought Portland would be different," said Wendy.

"This isn't Portland," I said. "This is the inside of my mom's brain."

There was a knock on the door. My mom appeared, holding a tray with glasses of milk and peanut butter and jelly sandwiches.

"YES! Snack time!" said Wendy.

"Don't," I said. "It's a trap!"

Wendy ignored me. She ate her sandwich and then my mom brought graham crackers and marshmallows and hot chocolate.

"I feel safe," said Wendy.

"This isn't the real world," I said.

"Can we live here forever?"

"Most of literature was written to warn us about this moment. Remember Goldilocks? Hansel and Gretel?"

Wendy pretended she couldn't hear me, licking the bottom of her ice cream bowl.

Wendy got a job at a coffee shop in the city, but no matter how many applications I submitted, nobody called me back. My dad repeated his offer to get me a job at his electrical contracting company on the condition that I cut my long red hair. Reluctantly, I agreed. I went into the bathroom, took a lock of hair between my fingers, and waited for the phone to ring. I waited and waited, but Angela didn't call asking me to go to Montana with her. Nobody interrupted or told me not to do it or said, "Hey, let's run away from this ridiculous place."

I squeezed, and a lock of hair fell into the sink in the shape of a bright orange question mark.

My job at Maloney Electric Co. consisted of driving a one-ton pickup truck to various job sites throughout the city, delivering tools and copper wire. I was bad at it. Even though I'd lived in the greater Portland area most of my life, I didn't know where anything was because I'd never paid attention to street names and landmarks because I assumed that when I grew up, I'd work as a writer or filmmaker or some other job where I spent my time being a reality-ignoring genius. Yet here I was, part of the actual world, a slave to the dollar, which I needed to liberate my girlfriend from her American Girl doll jail.

Every morning the shop manager loaded the truck with tools and handed me a list of parts to pick up from the electrical supply store, along with the job site I was supposed to deliver them to.

"I'll be back before you know it," I said.

I hopped in the truck and zipped around the city, ferrying wire cutters and MC cable to half-built office buildings in Gresham and Hillsboro.

Most of the time I found the job site after 30 minutes of driving around, but occasionally a Buffalo Springfield song came on the radio and I started thinking about the beautiful mountains and forests covering the earth, and the next thing I knew, I was sitting on a park bench next to the Willamette River, watching tugboats and oil tankers float by, thinking about how all of this used to belong to the American Indians.

It was around this time that I read J. Krishnamurti for the first time and started praying without ceasing, hoping to attain enlightenment. It made it difficult to drive a car, let alone a massive truck loaded with pipe benders and 500-pound job site boxes.

"OM," I said. "Shantih shantih shantih…"

"What's that?" asked the job foreman.

"I—uh. Here are your objects," I said, gesturing toward the back of the pickup truck.

"Hey, you're Wayne Maloney's son, aren't you?"

"I—I don't…"

I focused on my inbreath and mouthed the supplication of my guru. The foreman shook his head and returned to his blueprints.

On the drive back to the shop, mumbling my prayer, I watched the white line lift off the freeway and transform into a snake that slithered into my lap and tempted me to leave the Path of Knowledge.

"I will never abandon the Truth," I said.

"You already have," said the Highway Snake.

I reached out to strangle the malicious viper. A car honked, and I swerved back into my lane.

While I was fighting for my soul on the highways of greater Portland, Wendy was taking the bus back and forth to work and otherwise hiding from my mom. The initial joy of having her every need met had recently given way to paranoia that she was losing the ability to do things for herself.

"Cookie," Wendy said one day, extending her hand, expecting a cookie to magically appear. When it didn't, she became frustrated. She walked around the house saying, "Cookie! Cookie! Cookie!" over and over until she found a note from my mom explaining that she was at a doctor's appointment.

The idea of having to get a cookie for herself filled Wendy with rage, which made her realize that my mom had cast some sort of spell over her. She tracked down the cookies and made herself a peanut butter and jelly sandwich and stood in front of the mirror, saying, "You are a strong and capable woman. You are a strong and capable woman. You are a strong and capable woman."

Portland, Oregon, was an incredible place in the year 2000. Artists priced out of L.A. and San Francisco were astonished to discover that a room in a North Portland bungalow cost as little as $250 per month. They arrived in a mass exodus that eventually gentrified the city and displaced a historically Black neighborhood but, for a few years, gave birth to a thriving arts community featuring lumberjack-clad hipsters, tall bikes, and a Northeast Portland Craftsman occupied entirely by clowns.

We'd stumbled into all of this by accident and should have been out there staking our claim in this freakshow bonanza, but Wendy had fallen into a depression inextricably bound with the gray skies and endless rain of the Rose City.

We'd been in Portland for about two months when I came home from work and announced, "Hey, babe! We finally have enough money saved up. We should start our apartment hunt!"

Wendy peeked her head out of the closet. "Is your mom home?"

"She's at the grocery store."

"What about Molly?"

"Who?"

Wendy pointed to the doll shelf above our bed. Samantha, Kirsten, and Felicity were in their usual positions, but Molly was missing.

"What did you do with Molly?" I asked.

"*Me?*" said Wendy. "I didn't do anything. That bitch wouldn't stop staring at me!"

I searched the room and found an American Girl doll under the bed, mummified in duct tape with a dozen fondue skewers plunged into her abdomen.

I joined Wendy in the closet. There were candles burning and a dozen tarot cards arranged in the shape of a cross.

"I asked the deck what we should do," said Wendy. "It says we moved to the wrong Portland. We're cursed. To lift the curse, we have to move to Portland, Maine, and live by the ocean and eat lobster rolls and gaze at Canada all day, or whatever it is they do in that backwoods moose kingdom."

I said, "Are you being serious right now?"

She said, "You like lobster, right? Give me one good reason why we shouldn't move to Maine."

I could think of a thousand reasons, but this was my first real relationship, and I assumed it was my duty as boyfriend to agree to Wendy's every whim.

20

The Red Tent

Wendy and I used our apartment money to buy a 1991 Ford Tempo with 200,000 miles on it, piled our possessions in the backseat, and set out on a 3,000-mile journey to New England, which we'd fled two months earlier in a moment of boredom.

The other Portland was smaller and had more brick buildings and smelled like somebody left a salted cod on the sidewalk. We parked and walked around, orienting ourselves to our new city.

"It's kind of boring here, huh?" said Wendy. "I've never been in a city where I felt the constant need to yawn."

"We just got here," I said.

"It has bad energy," said Wendy. "I think I just don't like Portlands."

"What do you want to do?"

"Let's keep driving up the coast. We'll find something."

We continued up Highway 1, stopping in towns along the way so Wendy could do tarot readings so the universe would have a say in where we lived. She drew Death in Freeport, the Devil in Brunswick, the Tower in Waldoboro, and the Eight of Swords in

Rockland. Drifting into Belfast, Wendy pulled a card and held it up in the air. It depicted a goddess lounging in a field of wheat, wearing a crown made of stars.

"Is that good?" I asked.

"It's the Empress," said Wendy.

"Who's that?"

"Just like… the Queen of the Earth. Femininity, motherhood, creativity, abundance. It's pretty much the best card. The universe wants us to live in Belfast."

Wendy got hired as a waitress at a diner where the customers wore suspenders and rode snow mobiles and called their wives "Muhmuh." I got a job making sandwiches at the food co-op, spooning hummus onto sprouted bread for back-to-the-land, sandal-wearing flower children.

I wasn't one to doubt the Major Arcana, but Maine was weird. The locals were a hardy people embroiled in a decades-long feud re: whether Stihl or Husqvarna made a superior chainsaw. When they talked, they peppered their conversations with expressions like, "Ayuh" and "Wicked" and "You can't get theyuh from heyuh."

On a cool October morning, Wendy and I were walking down High Street when we noticed a commotion at the main intersection downtown. It was a Ford F-250 dragging a trailer upon which lay a dead moose with its enormous black tongue hanging out and a bullet hole in its brain. Instead of screaming in terror, everyone praised the dead animal's beauty. They took turns posing for photographs with the cadaver and placed bets guessing its weight.

I kept thinking, "We're in the wrong timeline. We're not supposed to be here."

I pictured our life back in Portland: drinking IPAs out of mason jars, attending art shows in renovated school buses, going to house shows where jug bands covered David Bowie's *The Rise and Fall of Ziggy Stardust* on washboard and kazoo.

Winter arrived, and with it, an ungodly amount of snow. Wendy and I didn't own a television. I don't think Netflix had been invented yet, or if it had, nobody told us. At night, we sat at a small table, drinking red wine and talking.

Without friends to distract us, we got annoyed by each other. Wendy fidgeted constantly, picking at her cuticles until her fingers were bloody stumps. I talked about how the guitarist for the Red Hot Chili Peppers was the greatest artist since Leonardo da Vinci. But there was nothing to do, so we had sex and smoked cigarettes and watched the smoke rise slowly to the ceiling as we blinked and tried to think of things we hadn't already told each other.

"This one time I stabbed my brother in the back with a fork," I said. "He deserved it."

"I know," said Wendy, blowing a smoke ring through another smoke ring. "You told me a thousand times."

"My favorite band is the Cocteau Twins," said Wendy.

"No shit," I said. "We're listening to them right now."

Eventually we fell silent.

The clock ticked on the wall.

A fly landed on the overhead light fixture and burned to death.

"I love you," I said.

"Cool," said Wendy.

Not much happened for three months. Wendy got better at blowing smoke rings. We listened to a lot of Cocteau Twins. I started feeling bad about stabbing my brother with a fork.

Then, in mid-April, the sun came out, and Wendy and I felt an optimism about life that we hadn't felt since the early days of our relationship when we used to stay up until 3 o'clock in the morning drunkenly debating whether *Plastic Ono Band* or *All Things Must Pass* was the best post-Beatles solo album.

"We should go to the beach," said Wendy.

"It's 28 degrees," I said.

"Quit being such a pussy."

We drove to Owls Head State Park and hiked through the snow to the snow-covered beach. Wendy stripped down to her striped bikini and waded out into the water.

"How is it?" I asked.

"I can't feel my feet," she said.

"This is a bad idea," I said.

For once, Wendy agreed with me. She put her clothes back on and wrapped a scarf around her face, and a piercing wind ripped through the air, freezing the moisture between my eyelashes.

"We should get hot toddies somewhere and sit by a fireplace," I said.

"It's beach day," said Wendy. "I'm not leaving the beach."

I found a half-eaten bag of Kettle chips in the pocket of my winter coat. We decided to have a picnic, but every time I laid the blanket on the snow, wind ripped across the sand, lifting the blanket into the air and tossing it into the ocean.

Eventually Wendy sat on it and wrapped it around her body and draped it over her head like a tent.

"Hey, stupid," she said. "Get in here."

I went inside the tent. Everything was red because the blanket was red. It was like a womb.

With a red face, Wendy said, "Is there anyone else on the beach?"

I looked through the tent flap. There wasn't. It was too cold. It was just us. I shook my head.

She took off her jeans and underwear and pointed at her pussy. "Quick, put your dick inside of me."

I didn't have a condom. We'd never done it without a condom before.

"It's fine," she said. "I'm outside my window."

I wasn't a hundred percent sure what window she was referring to, but I wasn't going to miss my chance. I did as I was told.

It was a thousand times more intimate than I expected, and scary, like I'd accidentally walked into a church where everyone was singing ecstatic songs to a god I didn't believe in.

On the drive home, I couldn't stop shaking. In part because I'd waded into the ocean a dozen times to fetch our blanket, but mostly because we'd crossed a frontier. I don't know what we were thinking. Probably we weren't thinking at all. There was a sense that any moment we might take out a small loan and buy an old barn. I'd use part of it as an art studio; Wendy would pick wild herbs and make tinctures and sell them at the co-op. We believed in magic and assumed we were living magical lives. In a way, we were.

A few nights later, Wendy and I got drunk and had sex without a condom, and a week after that we did it again.

There wasn't any more talk about windows. We were practicing an ancient form of birth control called "denial."

By May, it was warm enough to open our apartment windows. We celebrated by popping the cork on a bottle of chianti and drinking until we had purple teeth.

"If you were stranded on a deserted island—" I said, "—and could only bring five CDs, which CDs would you bring? I'll go first. Red Hot Chili Peppers *Blood Sugar Sex Magik* obviously. John Coltrane *A Love Supreme*. Neil Young *Decade*. Wait, does that count? It's sort of a best of—"

"I'm two weeks late," said Wendy.

"For what?" I asked.

"My period."

"That's normal, right?"

"Not really."

I started sweating. Never in my wildest dreams had it occurred to me that I could get my girlfriend pregnant by ejaculating inside of her pussy.

"What should we do?" I asked.

"We need a test."

We drove to the grocery store and bought a pregnancy test. Wendy took it in the bathroom. She lit a cigarette and started pacing as we waited for the results.

I got down on the floor and put my head between my legs and did a breathing exercise so I wouldn't pass out.

Wendy took a long drag from her cigarette, threw it in the toilet and said, "Shit!"

"What's it say?" I asked.

"Two pink lines."

"What does that mean?"

"It means we're going to have a baby."

PART III
HOLY MATRIMONY

21

Hopes and Dreams

My spiritual journey was obviously over, so I decided to abandon all my hopes and dreams in one dramatic gesture by asking Wendy to marry me. While she was at work, I drove to a jewelry store in Bangor and picked out a 2-carat engagement ring in 14K white gold. The jeweler asked what size Wendy's finger was.

I said, "I don't know. Regular. A little pudgy but not too pudgy."

He said, "Let's try a 7."

He put the ring in a velvet box and the velvet box in a velvet bag and the velvet bag in a paper bag.

"With tax," he said, "that comes to $11,875."

I dislodged a flax seed from my teeth, laughing at the idea of a human being having that much money.

He showed me the cheap rings. They started at $495.

I said, "How much for the velvet box?"

When Wendy got home from work, I was wearing a tie held together with a paper clip.

"What's wrong?" she asked.

"Put on a dress," I said. "We're going out to dinner."

We went to a fancy restaurant. I ordered a glass of wine. Wendy ordered water.

"Just so you know, I'm in a really bad mood," she said.

"Okay," I said.

"A 90-year-old snowmobile salesman hit on me today. He asked me to sit on his lap."

"Gross."

"My manager said, 'What's the problem? All the other waitresses sit on Henry's lap.'"

"That's awful, babe. I'm sorry."

"Men should be castrated at birth."

I fingered the velvet box in my pocket. This wasn't how I'd imagined our night going, but it was too late to back out. I got down on a knee, and the waiter appeared with our drinks.

"Let me tell you about tonight's specials," he said. "We have lobster ravioli with swiss chard and fried mushrooms. We also have an herb-crusted lamb with semolina gnocchi that's out of this world."

Wendy asked what the soup of the day was. The waiter couldn't remember so he went to the kitchen to find out.

"What are you doing on the floor?" asked Wendy.

"I want to ask you something," I said, reaching into my pocket.

"Would you judge me if I had a sip of your wine?"

"Go for it," I said. "Wait. Actually, no. Please don't drink wine. It's bad for the baby."

"Narc," said Wendy.

The waiter appeared and announced that the soup of the day was heirloom tomato bisque.

"Yum," said Wendy.

"Will you marry me?" I asked, opening the velvet box.

"Is that a hemp bracelet?" asked Wendy.

"It's a placeholder until I can afford a real engagement ring."

"Put that thing away," said the waiter. "You're embarrassing yourself."

"I love you so much," I said.

"Are you seriously asking me to marry you?" asked Wendy.

I nodded.

"You want to spend the rest of your life with me?"

I nodded.

She shrugged. "All right. Let's do it. Fuck it."

I was a 24-year-old hippie with long red hair and a mangy beard, outfitted in an undersized suit from the Salvation Army, standing in a gazebo, barefoot, about to be married. It didn't make any sense, but then again, neither did the baby growing inside Wendy's uterus—a slimy pink alien, half her, half me, created by sex, roughly the size of an ear of corn.

Wendy hadn't arrived yet. She'd run off somewhere with her sister, Peg. It was just our immediate families and a witch named Tree who performed tarot readings out of a ramshackle house on Highway 1 near Belfast. Wendy and I weren't religious, but we believed in eclipses and cloven-hooved animals, so we asked her to officiate our wedding.

Tree was dressed in a purple evening gown. No pointy hat. She was a classy witch.

"How's everybody doing?" she asked.

"Happy," said Marion, who looked terrified.

I opened my mouth to say something but started to throw up, so I closed my mouth.

Tree looked at her watch. "Bride's running a little late. No biggie."

My dad grinned, trying to pretend this was normal. My mom, high on drugs, didn't know what was happening. Terrified of flying so soon after the 9/11 disaster, she'd talked her psychiatrist into writing her a generous prescription for Diazepam. She gobbled up those pills like candy. For the last hour, she couldn't stop talking about the stained-glass windows even though we were standing outside in a public park next to a field of cows that smelled strongly of manure.

A rusty Buick pulled into the nearby parking lot. Its serpentine belt emitted a high-pitched screeching sound.

"Ooh. There they are!" said Tree.

Wendy stepped out of the passenger seat. She looked like a grocery store employee unloading a 50-pound bag of flour. The reason was her stomach. She was extremely pregnant.

When she finally freed that voluminous mound, I got a good look at the woman who was about to be my wife. Her hair was thinning at the temples and her teeth were too small and she had acne scars that made her cheeks look like raw hamburger, but I got dizzy seeing her in a white wedding dress with all those sequins and frills, thinking how lucky I was that she'd picked me to be her husband.

Tree pressed play on an old cassette player. It was Joni Mitchell's "Both Sides Now."

I started crying. I couldn't help it. I was the baby of the family. I didn't know how the stock market worked. But here I was, a man. Nearly a husband.

Tree gave a tasteful speech about full moons and the meaning of the corn sacrifice, then asked if I took Wendy to be my wife.

I said yes.

She asked Wendy if she took me to be her husband.

Wendy said yes.

Tree kept talking, but I listened to everything else: the ticking of my dad's watch, the horn of a boat out in the harbor, the low of a cow calling out to another cow in the adjacent pasture. Whatever we'd just become was inextricable from all that.

Thinking about the ways that I am a fucked up, unhealthy adult, near the top of the list is how often I think about my ex-wife's hair the day we were married. She had daisies woven through her wispy auburn locks. When she looked into my eyes as we took our vows, I couldn't breathe. She wasn't the prettiest girl I'd ever met, but I didn't want anybody else.

At some point during the ceremony, I blacked out. Not drunk but afraid. I just wanted to smoke pot and read Kurt Vonnegut novels and live in a shack made of wooden pallets and grow root vegetables, settling a longstanding argument with my father that you didn't need to work 40 hours a week for 30 years if you were crafty and reduced your needs and studied the *Bhagavad Gita*. But here I was, a husband and a father. It was too much. My brain shut off. After that, everything comes in snippets.

I remember Wendy's dad, a red-nosed alcoholic, discovering that my dad was picking up the tab at the reception. He ordered a triple vodka with another triple vodka on the side.

I remember my mom saying, "I'm so happy right now. Isn't everybody happy?"

Then suddenly it was over, and Wendy and I were in our hotel room. I wanted to make love as husband and wife, but Wendy said the baby kept kicking her in the heart, causing her to throw up in her esophagus.

We decided to take a bath instead. The tub was small. The only way we could fit was for Wendy to drape her legs over my legs.

It was a nice view. I couldn't believe I got to put my penis inside of this beautiful woman every day for the rest of my life.

"Quit looking at my pussy," said Wendy.

"What?" I asked.

"My pussy. You're staring at it. Stop."

"But you're my wife."

"That doesn't mean you get to look at it all the time. Jesus."

She covered herself with a washcloth.

Wendy still had daisies in her hair. Her nipples were enormous brown mushrooms. They scared me.

"I really want to make love right now," I said.

"I really want a cigarette," said Wendy.

She got out of the tub. The water level dropped to a couple inches. I started shivering.

Wendy pulled a pack of American Spirits out of her purse and lit one. She turned on the fan and waved her hand around, clearing the smoke.

"This is a non-smoking room," I said.

"I'm pregnant," said Wendy. "They make an exception when you're pregnant."

"I think it's the other way around."

"Just let me take a 10-minute break from having a baby inside of me, okay? I'm really stressed out."

Wendy finished her cigarette. We lay on the hotel bed, watching TV in our bathrobes. These were precious months when condoms weren't necessary, an accidental window created by me not wearing one when they were.

I wanted to watch a romantic comedy to get us in the mood, but Wendy insisted on *Law & Order: Special Victims Unit*. It was an episode about child sex trafficking. For 30 minutes, Ice-T conducted a manhunt in New York City, only to watch the perpetrator exonerated due to improper handling of evidence. We watched the local news and 30 minutes of David Letterman. Around midnight, we finally got around to consummating our marriage, but Wendy seemed distracted. Only now, all these years later, does it occur to me that she was terrified. She'd just married a man who made $8 an hour and thought the purpose of life was *burning for the ancient heavenly connection to the starry dynamo in the machinery of night*. She needed someone to tell her that everything was going to be okay. Instead, when she confessed how scared she was, I said, "Yeah, me too." I didn't know it was my job to lie to her.

22

The Texas Chainsaw Massacre

Instead of drinking tequila in a thatch-roofed bar on the shores of Puerto Vallarta, Wendy and I spent our honeymoon in the bedroom of our apartment, flipping through baby name books, trying to figure out what to name our child.

I liked Jennifer for a girl, but Wendy said with a name like that our daughter would end up working in finance one day, wearing polar fleeces and rock climbing on the weekends.

"Besides," said Wendy, "I'm like, 99 percent set on Jemima. I'd appreciate it if you just trust me on this."

I said, "Are you serious?"

She said, "It's a beautiful name. It's from the Bible."

I said, "What about the syrup?"

She said, "What about it?"

I said, "Isn't it kind of racist?"

She said, "Syrup can't be racist. I feel like you're being really aggressive right now."

We were having our first fight as husband and wife. I didn't like it. Based on watching 100,000 hours of television as a child, I was under the impression that marriage consisted of nonstop bliss periodically culminating in unbridled fornication.

I decided to make peace.

"Okay, fine," I said.

"Wait—really?" asked Wendy.

"It doesn't sound like I have a choice."

"Oh my God, this makes me so happy!"

Wendy wrote "Jemima Maloney" in fancy cursive on the first page of our Baby Memory Book.

She looked at it for a minute and said, "Hm. It's kind of racist, isn't it?"

I said, "I'm sure it'll be okay."

She said, "What about Zoë?"

I said, "Works for me."

Once a week, Wendy and I attended birthing classes in a yurt behind the treehouse of our midwife, Rain. We learned about chakras, drew pictures of our auras, and watched videos of beautiful vaginas becoming engorged by baby skulls until they exploded in discharges of blood and mucus.

In one video, a pregnant woman floating in a Plexiglas bathtub delivered her own baby while comforting her 2-year-old daughter, who watched the ordeal through the tub's window. As the woman spoke, the camera zoomed in on her vulva. First there was a triangle of hair; then an evil purple piglet shot out, turning the tub crimson with blood.

The expectant mothers in the room said things like, "What a badass!" and "That woman is my hero!" but the fathers were having a reckoning with all the *Hustler* magazines we'd gawked at in our youth. Larry Flynt was a liar. Women weren't airbrushed goddesses. Sex had consequences. Terrifying ones. I imagined a centerfold featuring a bloody placenta. A close-up of an epidural piercing a naked spine.

Another video came on. It was the same woman. She was having another baby. Two kids looked on: the same girl as before, only taller, and a little boy, presumably the piglet, now age 2. They pushed their faces up against the glass so they could meet their new piglet brother.

The woman sang a lullaby that gave way to a series of moans. Then her eyes rolled back in their sockets and *The Texas Chainsaw Massacre* started playing between her legs.

I covered my eyes and watched between my fingers. The baby popped out and swam around like Jacques Cousteau, inspecting the world through the Plexiglas while drinking oxygen through its umbilical cord. The older piglets waved at him. The baby waved back.

"What the fuck is happening?" I yelled, standing up.

I couldn't tell what was real anymore. I started pacing the room. I thought I'd get in trouble for making a commotion, but the other expectant parents were revolting too.

"What have you done to us?" said an indignant pregnant teen. "I can't unsee that!"

"She's not my hero anymore," said Wendy.

Rain pressed pause. She was crying. "Isn't it beautiful?"

One of the dads got up to use the bathroom. Another lit a cigarette.

"Not all of your births will be as transcendent as Anastasia's," said Rain. "But I promise, no matter how intense the pain or how long the contractions, it will be a gift from the goddess."

23

The Mesozoic Era

One morning I was getting ready for work when Wendy yelled at me from the kitchen, accusing me of spilling water all over the floor. I peeked my head around the corner and discovered Wendy frantically mopping up liquid that was shooting out of her body.

"You're such a slob!" she said. "What are we going to do when we have a baby? Do I have to clean up after both of you?"

"Hey, Wendy—" I said.

"Are you even listening?" she sobbed. "I can't keep doing this. You're a grown man. I need you to clean up after yourself. If you're feeling really ambitious, maybe run a load of dishes? I know—crazy, right?"

The water kept gushing from between her legs, forming pools around her slippers.

"Wendy—" I said.

"You know what? I don't want this baby anymore. Is it too late for an abortion?"

"I think your water broke," I said.

She snarled at me, then looked down at the floor.

"I think my water broke," she said.

"It's fine," I said. "Everything's going to be fine."

"No, it isn't."

"I'll call the midwife."

"I hate you so much."

I called Rain and told her that Wendy was in labor and to please come over so I could start breathing again.

"That's wonderful!" said Rain. "But I should caution you, this is just the beginning. Try to relax. Go for a walk. Call me when things feel unbearable."

Wendy put on a winter parka. We went outside and tried to walk around the neighborhood, but it was covered in 2 feet of fresh-fallen snow. Every few steps, Wendy grabbed my arm and made me promise that we'd never have sex ever again, no matter how horny we got.

"It isn't worth it," she said. "What if every time you masturbated, you had to push a guinea pig out of your dick?"

"It's not the same thing," I said.

"Oh, it isn't?" said Wendy. "When did you become an expert on women's reproductive health? Because last time you went down on me, I seem to remember you fumbling around down there like you dropped a jellybean under the couch. But no… please, by all means, tell me how giving birth isn't the same thing as—whoopsie daisy!"

Wendy slipped on an ice patch and fell into a snowbank. I picked her up.

"This doesn't feel right," I said. "I don't think Rain knows what she's doing."

"It's fine," said Wendy.

"It doesn't feel fine."

A guy on cross-country skis passed us, followed by two huskies towing a toboggan captained by a mail carrier wearing a fur-lined aviator hat.

Wendy took a few more steps, then got down on her hands and knees and said, "Oh boy, here we go! Baby's coming!"

She unbuttoned her bib and started peeling it off.

"Stop!" I said. "You can't have the baby on the sidewalk!"

"Too late," she said, pulling down her underwear.

Cars slowed and rolled down their windows.

"Ugggggghhhhhhhh!!!!!!!!" moaned Wendy. "Is it a boy or girl?"

"It didn't come out," I said.

"Are you serious? I felt a baby come out."

I looked around, but there wasn't a baby in the snow.

Wendy put her bib back on, and we walked back to the apartment.

I called Rain and told her Wendy was in labor for real this time and that the baby was halfway out of her vagina.

Rain said, "Is the baby actually halfway out of her vagina?"

I said, "No, but it feels that way."

She said, "These things take time. Call me when she's in actual distress."

I looked at Wendy. She was half submerged in an inflatable birthing tub, naked, chewing on the wooden arm of a rocking chair she'd ripped off during her last contraction. I wasn't an expert, but it felt like she'd moved way beyond "distress." I held the phone up so Rain could hear the sound Wendy was making.

Rain said, "What is that? Is that a moose?"

I said, "That's Wendy."

She said, "I'm coming right over."

Before I got off the phone, Rain said that if the baby was born before she got there to make sure the umbilical cord wasn't wrapped around its neck and to keep the airway clear and to swaddle it to keep it warm.

I said, "Sounds good," only it didn't sound good. I was the opposite of a doctor. Whenever I saw blood, tiny orbs floated across my field of vision and I had to sit on the floor with my head between my knees to keep from passing out.

I interrupted one of Wendy's contractions to ask her if any part of the baby had come out yet.

Instead of answering, she hissed and swiped at me with her fingernails and said, "No sounds. Shhhhhh."

I said, "It's my duty as your husband to check your cervix," and climbed into the tub with her.

Wendy grabbed my arm and twisted the skin in opposite directions, the exact same move my brother performed on me after I stabbed him in the back with a fork.

It was pretty clear Wendy had no intention of letting me perform even a cursory examination of her vagina, so I decided to write a poem instead. I found a notepad and a pen and started composing a stream of consciousness poem inspired by Jack Kerouac, a Beat writer famous for his misogynistic accounts of glorified men-children.

The poem went, *Holy shit my wife is in labor right now a baby is about to come out of her vagina any second this is the most psychedelic thing that has ever happened to me. I feel like the universe is—*

"What's that sound?" asked Wendy.

"What sound?" I said.

"*Scritch-scritch-scritch.*"

"It's my pen."

"Why?"

"I'm writing a poem."

"Make it stop."

I was offended. Wendy, my so-called muse, had zero respect for the beautiful work of art I was creating about the baby she was giving birth to. It was typical of her that she'd only think about herself at a moment like this. The poem was good. One of my best. I decided to go outside and finish it.

I'd filled two and a half pages with inspired hallucinatory prose when a Subaru pulled up covered with divine goddess bumper stickers.

"How dilated is she?" asked Rain.

"Three centimeters," I said, which sounded like it could be true.

"Excellent," she said. "You did a good job."

The midwife was right. Wendy wasn't even close to giving birth. When she rushed inside with her medical bags, she found Wendy in the birthing tub, drinking sparkling water out of a champagne flute and watching an episode of *Seinfeld* on a portable TV.

Rain said, "What's going on? I thought you were having a baby."

Wendy said, "I thought I was, and then suddenly I wasn't. It's confusing."

Rain asked whether Wendy's contractions hurt more when she was in the tub or on dry land.

Wendy said, "Dry land. Definitely. It feels amazing in here."

Rain made her get out of the tub, which made Wendy snarl and hiss at her, and I started crying from happiness that Wendy was snarling and hissing at somebody other than me.

Rain went to the store to buy green tea and snacks, and Wendy and I went into the bedroom and sat on the bed.

Wendy said, "This sucks. I liked the tub better. I'm going to lie and say it hurt more in the tub."

I said, "I don't think it's a good idea to lie."

Wendy said, "Whatever, *Dad*. Do you want to have this baby for me?"

I said, "I would if I could."

She said, "You are literally the most annoying person I've ever met."

A contraction started, and I tried to hold Wendy's hand, but she told me that if I ever touched her again, she'd remove my testicles with a melon baller while I was sleeping, so I let go.

At some point, Wendy's body emitted a powerful hormone that caused the three of us who weren't having a baby—myself, Rain, and Rain's assistant Astrid, who'd just arrived from a Wiccan ceremony and who appeared to be outfitted in the crimson robe of a high priestess—to fall into a profound sleep, the sort I hadn't experienced since I was a child. I dreamed it was the Mesozoic Era. Titanic ferns burst from the volcanic soil with an audible shrieking sound. A stegosaurus thundered across the landscape, swinging its plated tail like a bored and violent god. The earth trembled as the continents ripped apart, still grooved like the puzzle pieces of Pangea.

When I woke up, I heard a primitive cry born out of the dream I'd just had. I ran to the living room and found Wendy back in the tub and the room filled with burning candles. Wendy's pupils were gone; her eyes were completely white. She moaned as if possessed. Rain and Astrid—no longer dawning the robe of her ceremony—were different people. There was a black valise open on the floor. Stainless steel surgical tools were lined up on a piece of cloth. Out of Wendy's field of vision, these earth goddesses were quietly transforming our apartment into an operating room.

I got on my knees and hovered over the birthing tub. Wendy didn't think to scowl because she wasn't here with the rest of us on Planet Earth. She let out a fierce moan, and her stomach changed shape before our eyes as our child began to leave it. There was a plume of blood, and a purple baby floated up to the surface of the water.

My hand shook too bad to cut the umbilical cord, so the midwife cut it for me and wrapped Zoë in a blanket and handed her to me.

Wendy tried to get out of the tub but got dizzy and slipped. Blood rushed down her thighs. While the midwives conferred, trying to figure out how to sew her back together, I gazed down into my baby's blue eyes and prayed to Jesus to please let my family be healthy and not die.

I remember the feeling of Zoë's limbs moving inside her swaddling clothes. Her pathetic cry and the unexpected love I felt for this helpless pink thing. I didn't know what to do with a newborn baby, so I took her outside. I pointed at the trees and said, "Sweetheart, those are trees." I pointed at the clouds and said, "Those are clouds." I pointed at the sky and said, "That's the universe. We're on a planet. It's spinning around the sun. I don't understand it either."

Zoë's eyes were wide open. I didn't know babies could see only minutes after being born. I looked into them, those tiny blue puddles.

What I want to know, what I keep wanting somebody to tell me all these years later, is—can you really move on from a moment like that? Or can you stay there for the rest of your life, holding your baby girl, kissing the top of her skull over and over, the soft part that wasn't formed yet with its earthy smell like the part of Wendy I entered to make that tiny perfect creature?

Does anybody know? And if you do, and the answer is what I think it is—will you please let me stay here just a few more minutes?

24

Queen of Dandelions

For a few days, Wendy and I sat around looking at our baby, totally amazed by the thing we made by accident, having unprotected sex in a makeshift tent on an abandoned beach. But a week later Zoë was still there. I'd assumed that an adult would show up at some point to take care of her so Wendy and I could get back to drunkenly debating whether *Plastic Ono Band* or *All Things Must Pass* was the best post-Beatles solo album. But nobody showed up. We were the adults.

Between the two of us, we had the following life skills: making amazing mixtapes, praying without ceasing, writing poetry at inappropriate moments, and moving across the country for no reason.

Now we had a whole new set of skills to learn. Practical endeavors like cleaning liquid shit out of Zoë's forearm crevices and not quitting my job because I had a momentary urge to live in a teepee.

While Wendy swaddled Zoë and nursed her and attended to her every need, I sat in a rocking chair, reading *What to Expect the First Year*, a parenting book Wendy asked me to read months ago, which I was just getting around to reading now that we had a baby.

"Oh dang," I said. "We need a car seat."

"We already have one," said Wendy.

"It has to be backward-facing," I said.

"I know. It is."

"Did you know you can't feed babies honey?"

"Yes."

"That's fucked up. Wait—it says here we have to take Zoë to the doctor for regular checkups. Do we even have a doctor?"

Wendy said if I really wanted to be helpful, I'd invent a time machine and go back six months and read the book when she originally asked so she didn't have to be the one making all the decisions.

I got frustrated and went outside. I wanted to quit my job and live in a teepee. But I couldn't. Apparently, Thoreau never had sex. Either that or his girlfriend wasn't in her window.

I decided to make all my problems go away, so I sat on the sidewalk in the lotus position and touched my thoughts lightly with a feather every time they interrupted my bliss. First, I thought about Zoë screaming all the time and never sleeping. I said "thinking" and touched it lightly with a feather. Then I thought about how mean Wendy was and how I wished she used a nicer tone of voice when she was yelling at me. I said "thinking" and touched it lightly with a feather.

I repeated the process 10 more times and then my eyes crossed, and my mind went *zoop!* and the trees on the other side of the street looked like the shrubs in the background of *Super Mario Bros.*

"Holy shit," I thought. I'd achieved enlightenment. I knew I was close, but here it was. Wow. Cool. I wondered if they'd make a new religion about me or if they'd make me the saint of an already existing religion, and if so, which one? My first choice was Buddhism. Second choice Hinduism, followed by Christianity, but only if they made me cool, like Joan of Arc or Francis of Assisi.

I was trying to decide whether to ascend to heaven or stay here on earth as a bodhisattva when the sound of a screaming baby pierced my inner sanctuary. I said "thinking," but it wouldn't go away. I said "thinking," but it wouldn't go away.

Eventually I went inside and found Wendy crying and Zoë crying, and I started crying, and from then on, our family was miserable all the time, because you couldn't touch a baby with a feather and make it go away.

To help us adjust to being new parents, my mom flew across the country and moved in with us. It was a mistake. From the moment she arrived, she started following Wendy and Zoë around wherever they went, including the bathroom, trying to make eye contact with her granddaughter. She treated her like a celebrity, taking hundreds of photographs and whispering incomprehensible gibberish like, "Well, aren't you the cutest little Boo Bear ever?"

When Wendy finally asked for a little space, my mom started sobbing and checked into a hotel. I went over there to see if she was okay and found her hyperventilating and snorting lines of Valium. She flew home the next day.

The following week Wendy's mom, Marion, came for a visit. She poked Zoë in the arm and said, "What a fat little baby." Then she lit a cigarette.

Wendy said, "Mom! You can't smoke around the baby."

Marion rolled her eyes. "Give me a break. It's just smoke. It's fine."

Marion set up a yoga studio in our living room. Whenever Zoë cried, she said, "Can you tell her to keep it down? I'm nailing this mermaid pose. It requires all my concentration."

Later that night she put on hoop earrings and said she was going on a date.

"With who?" asked Wendy.

"The manager from the store where I bought Zoë's stuffed llama. His name's Jackson. He's an Aries. Wish me luck."

She didn't come home that night. A few days later, Marion left a message on our answering machine, saying that she and Jackson were in Acapulco and to send her love to "Zadie."

After two weeks paternity leave, I returned to work and discovered that my job, which I'd once regarded as an oppressive form of torture invented by capitalist overlords, was actually an oasis from the far more oppressive demands of raising a child. While Wendy trafficked in shit and screams, I made tempeh sandwiches for scantily clad earth goddesses who lingered about the deli, strumming ukuleles and gossiping about the dharma.

"Would you like pickles on your tempeh Reuben?" I asked.

"Sure," said the goddesses.

"Nutritional yeast?"

"Why not?"

After a cushy six-hour shift, I drove home and found Wendy sitting at the kitchen table, sobbing. Zoë was lying in a pile of laundry, screaming so violently she was projectile vomiting onto our linens.

I said, "What's going on here?"

Wendy said, "I want to kill our baby."

I said, "No, you don't."

She said, "Yes, I do."

I said, "You just think you do, but you don't really."

Wendy's eyes were bloodshot. She looked scared. "I… can't… do this."

At least, that's what I think she said. I couldn't hear anything. Zoë was screaming too loud.

I picked my daughter off the living room floor and carried her outside. We walked around the block three times, but she wouldn't stop crying. I bounced her on my shoulder and tickled her, but she wouldn't stop crying.

I tried my best rendition of "Hush, Little Baby," but partway through I took a wrong turn and found myself singing "Enter Sandman" by Metallica. It wasn't a good lullaby. Zoë didn't think so either. She took a shit in her diaper and puked in my hair and screamed so violently she turned purple and passed out.

For a few seconds, she was limp in my arms, which was almost the same as sleep, but I worried she wasn't getting any oxygen in her brain.

When she returned to consciousness, she was so scared at having fainted she forgot to cry and just looked at me.

"Why do you scream all the time?" I asked. "Whatever it is, I'll try to fix it."

Her eyes were full of water. She didn't speak English. Probably she didn't want to be born and I screwed everything up by having sex with her mom.

"She invited me inside the tent," I said. "She told me to do it. If it's any consolation, I don't understand why I'm alive either."

Zoë tried to cry, but she was too tired. She fell asleep. I walked through the neighborhood as slow as I could, trying to make the moment last forever.

With Zoë's head on my shoulder and baby drool cascading down my neck, it occurred to me for the first time that the meaning of life might not be zigzagging back and forth across the country for no reason or zapping your brain on magic mushrooms, but this: loving something so much it scares you, as you begin the slow, inevitable process of turning into your father.

Sometimes Zoë stopped crying for a few hours and we became a normal family with a normal baby living normal lives, and I could almost understand the appeal of the American dream— driving back and forth to work every day, buying a house, mowing the lawn, falling asleep watching TV, just to do it all over again the next day. But then a shadow flitted across Zoë's field of vision, and she started screaming, and I realized that the trappings of Western civilization were just narcotics for depressed parents pretending they hadn't made the worst mistake of their lives.

One day we were driving home from the grocery store, completely out of our minds. Zoë was in the backseat, crying and throwing up on herself. Wendy had her seatbelt off and was leaning between the driver's seat and passenger seat with her breast hanging out, trying to squirt a jet of milk into Zoë's screaming mouth.

I started having a panic attack, but then I remembered the teachings of J. Krishnamurti and started praying without ceasing.

"OM," I said. "Shantih shantih shantih…"

Wendy said, "What's that sound? You aren't praying without ceasing, are you?"

I said, "It helps with my nerves. I started having a panic attack, but now it's going away."

She said, "Please stop."

Wendy couldn't get Zoë to stop crying which made Wendy cry which made Zoë cry even louder which caused Zoë's projectile vomit to shoot even further into the front seat.

Wendy said, "I can't take this anymore. Pull over!"

I pulled into a gas station parking lot. I was worried Wendy was going to murder our baby, but she just unbuckled her from her car seat and nursed her.

Zoë cried and sucked and choked and spit up and screamed and threw up and inexplicably fell asleep.

I looked down at my fingers. I hadn't let go of the steering wheel. My knuckles were totally white, without any blood in them.

"Is it supposed to be this hard?" asked Wendy.

"I don't know," I said. "I don't think so."

"Do you think I'm a bad mother?"

"No. You're a good mother. You're the best."

"What am I doing wrong?"

She really wanted to know. Her lower lip trembled. She started to say something, but then a look of elation came over her face, and she laughed in the crazed, carefree manner of someone who, after a long period of distress, has completely lost their mind.

"Oh my God," she said. "We should buy cigarettes."

"But we quit," I reminded her.

"Did we though?"

I went into the gas station and bought a pack of American Spirits. When I got back to the car, Wendy was standing in a field, laughing and crying, plucking dandelions out of the earth. She wove them into a crown and placed it on her head.

"I'm the queen!" she sang. "I'm the Queen of Dandelions!"

I lit a cigarette and gave it to her. She took a deep drag. I lit one for myself and took a deep drag. We both started laughing. I made a crown of my own. I was the King of Dandelions. We were out of our minds, but the nicotine made us feel like serene geniuses.

Zoë was in the car, asleep or dead. She looked like a normal baby. She looked beautiful. A ray of sunlight fell on her sleeping pink face. She was an angel. Only she wasn't. She was a monster.

Wendy reached for my hand and squeezed it. I squeezed back.

Between puffs she said, "Smoking this cigarette is the most important thing I've done in my entire life."

I took a deep drag and said, "Same."

We went home and put Zoë in the Johnny Jump Up and pressed play on a *Baby Einstein* video. A cow sock puppet rang a triangle and an instrumental version of "Old McDonald Had a Farm" began playing over a montage of stock farm imagery.

Wendy and I snuck into the bedroom. She pulled her pants down and said, "Put your dick in me before I change my mind."

It had been a long time. I didn't hesitate.

Just when things were getting good, a talking sock in the *Baby Einstein* video moved too fast and Zoë started screaming.

"Do you need to check on her?" I asked.

"Shhhh!" said Wendy. "I want to finish."

"She sounds distressed."

"She's just a baby."

Wendy had an orgasm and I had an orgasm and then Wendy got out of bed and gave Zoë a banana even though she'd never eaten solid foods before.

We snuck outside and lit another cigarette. Drawing the smoke deep into our lungs, we watched the grass turn green and the flowers turn yellow and the sky transform into a new thing we'd never seen before, so blue it hurt to look at.

Wendy and I laughed and held hands. We hated our baby. It was something we had in common. Except we loved her more than anything. We had that in common too. We were in the jungles of Vietnam, smoking in a foxhole, waiting for Death to come, only Death was a baby.

It was fine. Everything was fine. Only it wasn't. We had a shrieking, shitting roommate we were required by law to take care of, whose greatest talent was eroding our will to live.

We finished our cigarettes and went inside and rewound the *Baby Einstein* video and started it over from the beginning.

We were bad parents, but it didn't matter because we were insane from lack of sleep and nothing mattered. We were ruining Zoë's life, and she was ruining ours.

25

Ten Dollar Bill

Wendy decided the problem wasn't the insomniac parasite who crawled out of her vagina and took us hostage with the power of her vocal cords, but Maine—the state we'd moved to because of a tarot reading Wendy did in a closet while she was hiding from an American Girl doll. She suggested we move back to Vermont where we still had friends who could babysit and commiserate as we aged prematurely and lost our minds.

I wasn't excited to move for the 11th time in three years, but as Wendy described her plan, her hands were shaking, and she kept laughing uncontrollably. There was breastmilk on her cheek and baby shit in her hair, and she was wearing a pair of inside-out overalls.

I said, "Whatever you need, sugar. I just want you to be happy."

We broke our lease, piled our possessions into our car, and drove to Burlington. It was the same as before, only different. When I'd arrived a few years earlier, the city felt like a bohemian paradise teeming with painters and poets who sipped Americanos in dimly lit cafes. Now it revealed itself to be a depressing college town full of unemployed vagrants.

We found an apartment in the Old North End and decorated it with Art Nouveau posters and bookshelves full of obscure Russian novels. In a rare moment of whimsy, we decided to adopt a cat, only to remember we already had a cat—Humphrey, whom we'd left with our friend Sam when we moved to Oregon.

The co-op gave me my old job back. The customers were the same as before. They said, "Hey! You've been gone a while! How's life?"

I said, "Yesterday. I was—but before. And then."

They waited for me to finish, but every time I blinked, my eyes stayed closed and I started to have a dream.

They said, "Is everything okay?"

I said, "What—what state are we in?"

They said, "Vermont."

I said, "No. That was before. We're somewhere else now."

They said, "This is definitely Vermont. You work at the co-op."

I said, "That was the past."

They said, "When's the last time you slept?"

I tried counting on my fingers, but every time I got past one, I forgot what I was doing.

I started laughing and sobbing, and then another cashier came over and finished the transaction.

At some point, Zoë stopped breastfeeding and started sleeping through the night. She learned to say "Mama" and "Dada" and "Ditty," which was her toddler's attempt at saying "Kitty," meaning Humphrey. Then she turned two; certain important wires connected in her brain, and she began speaking in fully formed sentences, directing my attention to her "fuzziest" sweater and her "all-time favorite" stuffed animal, as if she hadn't been an amniotic seahorse two summers ago.

With the return of sleep, Wendy and I felt a degree of normalcy returning to our lives. We went to the movies and planted a garden and took Zoë to the park and stood around, saying things like: "God, isn't she amazing? I can't believe we made such a beautiful, perfect kid!" But the second one of us put Zoë to bed, we retreated to different rooms and led separate lives.

One night after dinner, I pointed out to Wendy that we were about 90 percent of the way to being a happily married couple. The only thing left to do was start having some form of sex.

Wendy said, "We have sex."

I said, "When?"

She said, "That time in Maine. We put on the *Baby Einstein* video."

I said, "That was a year and a half ago."

She said, "Whatever. Our problem isn't sex; our problem is that we're poor."

I said, "We're not poor."

She said, "We have $2.37 in our checking account."

I said, "I get paid Friday."

She said, "It's Saturday. You got paid yesterday. We spent all the money."

I put my hand in my pocket and pulled out a Subway punch card. There were 3 out of 10 stamps toward a free sub.

"This has to be worth something," I said.

Wendy asked if I remembered Jim Foster, the guy who used to run the Health & Beauty Aid department at the co-op.

I said, "The one you had sex with because he has a high body temperature?"

Wendy said, "That's him. I ran into Jim at the library. Apparently, he owns his own yoga studio now. The receptionist is going on maternity leave and they need a part-time assistant to take her place. It's only temporary, but he says there's a chance it'll turn into a permanent position. He asked if I was interested. I said yes."

I didn't understand. For the last five years, I'd dedicated my life to earning as little money as possible to avoid the trappings of capitalism so I could spend my days outside, close to the earth, observing the serene movements of ladybugs. Yet here was Wendy, my so-called "wife," procuring work with the intention of improving our overall financial picture.

"Good luck with that," I said.

I walked outside, slammed the door, and looked up at the sky. Dumb birds were flying all around, making pathetic tweeting sounds. They weren't pretty. The clouds looked like decapitated rabbits and the sky was blue—an awful color I'd despised since the day I was born.

I sat down in the grass and took off my shoes. My toes had hair on the knuckles, squiggly orange things nobody wanted to look at. No wonder Wendy never wanted to have sex with me.

I lay down and waited to see if a car would veer off the road and kill me, but it didn't. I counted to 100, but I was still alive, so I started considering the possibility that I was wrong about everything. For instance: money. What if it wasn't the root of evil but a useful symbol representing work done on behalf of others, which you exchanged for goods and services? What if I'd been avoiding the very thing that would make me happy, based on a handful of trippy drug experiences and the counterfeit wisdom of a vegetable-loving charlatan squatting near Walden Pond?

I thought about a $10 bill I'd found the other day in the co-op parking lot. Instead of spending it on diapers or groceries, I'd gone to the record store and bought a Joy Division CD. Listening to it, I felt depressed in a way that made me feel elated. Money bought happiness. The philosophers were wrong!

For the first time since I started smoking again, I felt optimistic about life. I was going to get a job that made a lot of money. Good thing I had a college degree! No wait—I seemed to remember dropping out of college so I could dedicate my life to stacking apple cider vinegar bottles into geometric towers. I'd always thought of that as the best decision I'd made in my entire life, but now it occurred to me that I'd been on a wild goose chase for the last seven years, seeking nirvana with a bunch of lowlifes, while my peers were driving back and forth to work every day, buying houses, and investing in the stock market.

I sat upright.

A car drove by.

It didn't swerve off the road and kill me.

I decided to go back to college.

26

The Pea War

Mount Mansfield College was a humble state school with an adult education program that allowed working parents to complete their introductory courses online or evenings at the community college. The students had names like Hank, Sharon, and Billy. They'd spent their summers working as truck drivers and middle school janitors. Instead of wandering around campus, listening for the drunken laughter of keg dwellers, they applied themselves to their coursework, hoping a high GPA would translate into lucrative job opportunities when they graduated.

I switched from the afternoon to the morning shift at the co-op. From 6 a.m. to noon, I unloaded couscous and artichoke hearts from delivery trucks, then rushed home to relieve Wendy so she could rush off to her job at the yoga studio where she worked until 6 p.m., at which point she rushed home to relieve me so I could rush off to my trigonometry class at the community college.

Most nights I ate alone in the cafeteria, but one night my math class got cancelled and I made it home in time for dinner. Wendy was standing at the stove cooking soup. I snuck up behind her and planted a passionate kiss on her neck. She scowled. She was in a mood. I hadn't cleaned Humphrey's litter box in six months, an act of civil disobedience I hoped would call attention to all the sex we weren't having. It wasn't working. Rather than see the hurt feelings and desire for connection behind my childish refusal to do chores, Wendy doubled down, withholding all forms of affection, including a basic hello when I walked through the front door.

We ate dinner in silence. Halfway through, Zoë, sensing the tension permeating our family meal, loaded a single green pea onto her fork and, in a catapult maneuver known to everyone over the age of two, sent that little green orb in the direction of Wendy's head, missing by only a few inches.

"What the hell!" yelled Wendy. "Stop that!"

Zoë started crying. I felt bad for her. Wendy didn't know it, but her voice had the effect of making everyone in the room feel like horrible failures.

I didn't want Zoë to feel that way, so I loaded a pea onto my fork and shot it at Wendy. My aim was better—it hit her in the face. Zoë laughed so hard mashed potatoes came out of her nose.

Wendy stormed away from the table, accusing us of "ganging up on her" and "making her the enemy."

When she was gone, Zoë loaded even more peas onto her fork and launched them at me. We had a war. It was funny for a while, and then suddenly it wasn't.

"Time to stop," I said.

Zoë launched a pea at me.

"Honey, that's it. Game over."

She launched another pea. "Laugh!"

"Honey, please stop—"

"Laugh!" she commanded.

I laughed, but she wasn't satisfied. She started throwing peas around the kitchen, and I ran around picking them up.

After dinner Zoë wanted to watch more TV. Since Wendy had locked herself in the bedroom and I didn't know how to maintain boundaries, I said sure. I queued up *Dora the Explorer*, but Zoë said, "No, grownup TV!"

I turned on the evening news. It was a report about an earthquake in Pakistan. More than 80,000 people were believed dead. A long panoramic shot showed rivers of blood drooling out of massive heaps of rubble.

Zoë started screaming. I tried to change the channel, but I wasn't fast enough. Wendy came into the room, sobbing. She said she just needed a five-minute break from being a parent without me showing our daughter gory news footage.

It was close to Zoë's bedtime, so I tucked her into bed and read from her favorite book, Richard Scarry's *What Do People Do All Day?*

While I described the vocations of cats and dogs who lived in an idealized zoo world, Zoë tried to find the golden bug on every page.

At one point, I said, "Sweetheart, do you know what Daddy's job is?"

She said, "Firefighter!"

I shook my head.

She said, "Construction worker?"

I shook my head.

She said, "I don't know!"

I said, "I work at a grocery store."

She put her finger in her nose and fell asleep.

"Man, what a night," I said, crawling into bed with Wendy. "I know I encouraged her with that whole pea business, but she really lost control. It took forever, but I finally got her to sleep."

Wendy turned up the volume on the TV. It was *Law & Order SVU*.

"Hey!" I said. "This is the show we watched on our wedding night."

"Please be quiet," said Wendy.

Ice-T chased a pedophile down an alleyway, but the pedophile got away. The show went to commercial.

"Remember after the wedding when we took a bath and you still had flowers in your hair?" I said. "You looked so pretty."

"I'm really tired," said Wendy. "Can we just watch the show?"

"It's a commercial."

"Yeah. I'm curious about this product though."

We learned about Glad sandwich bags and a new flavor of Snapple and a local furniture company where you could buy everything on credit. The show came back on. Ice-T chased a pedophile down an alleyway and caught him this time. I got up and went outside and lit a cigarette.

I started to worry I'd made a mistake going back to college. What if Wendy and I were unhappy not because we were poor, but because we didn't love each other and never had and the only reason we were together was because our birth control consisted of crossed fingers and a mumbled prayer?

A shooting star flew across the sky. I made a wish, but then it flew back the other direction and I realized it was a moth.

I made a wish anyway. I wished that when I went back inside Wendy would run her fingers up and down my chest, saying, "I want you so bad, Kevin. I miss you. I want you inside of me."

I put out my cigarette and went inside. The TV was off. Wendy was asleep.

27

Wile E. Coyote

Being sexually rejected summoned a wave of complex emotions that I dealt with by drinking alcohol and trying to write a novel. My plan was to turn the 25-page mess I'd managed to cobble together in periodic fits of loneliness into a coherent manuscript that I'd sell to a major publishing house for a million dollars and begin the life I'd always dreamed of: sitting in a mahogany chair all day, stringing words together with such profundity that people wept and laughed and turned the pages of my books in desperation to find out whether the protagonist I'd created lived or died. I imagined a compendium of work that would outlive me, so that when I croaked and my grandchildren asked, "What was Pappy like when he was young?" Zoë could hand them a stack of my books and say, "He was a troubled soul."

That was the idea, but every night when I started writing, I immediately described the breasts and vaginas of my female characters in unnecessary detail. The breasts were always "perky," while the vaginas were "cavernous" and "moist." Then a male character walked into the room, and for no reason, throbbing, veiny cocks whirred across the blue sky like airplanes, dropping loads of semen on unsuspecting nuns.

I wrote for an hour or two, then gave up and went back to bed. I tried to stay on my side, but I was consumed by the erection I'd been harboring since Wendy and I started fooling around in our sleep a few weeks earlier, when Wendy woke up and said, "Oh shit. I was dreaming you were someone else. Disregard. I'm going back to bed."

Since then, the only thing that passed between us were hostile words and icy glares.

Slowly, like a perverted ninja, I reached my hand over and touched parts of Wendy I hadn't touched in months. There were damp places and hair and nipples that perked up when I moved my fingers around in vigorous circles.

"What are you doing?" asked Wendy.

"I don't know," I said.

"Please stop," she said.

"Okay," I said.

Wendy thought that if we ignored our problems for long enough, they'd go away on their own and we'd find ourselves in love again just like in the beginning. But I was impatient. I made us an appointment with a marriage counselor.

Wendy sat on the far end of the sofa, as far away from me as she could get without sitting on the floor. Dr. Hodson opened a small notebook and asked why we'd decided to seek counseling.

"Well, for one thing he never cleans the litter box," said Wendy. "It's the only chore I ask him to take responsibility for and he never does it."

"That's not true," I said.

"When's the last time you cleaned it—"

"Yesterday," I said.

"—without me reminding you?"

I opened my mouth, but no words came out.

Dr. Hodson raised his hand and said, "What I'm hearing you say, Wendy, is that you want Kevin to contribute to the household, but you feel like he isn't making it a priority. Does that sound accurate?"

Wendy nodded so vigorously her head almost popped off.

"This isn't about the litter box," I said. "Look—can we address the elephant in the room? Wendy and I have only had sex once since Zoë was born."

"Oh, here we go," said Wendy.

"What? Why can't we talk about this?"

Dr. Hodson raised his hand. Wendy made a face like she was going to bite one of his fingers off. The doctor lowered his hand.

"It's been *two years*," I said.

"Stop pressuring me," said Wendy.

"Two years! How is that pressure?"

"I have to go to the bathroom," said Wendy.

She got up and left the room. Dr. Hodson smiled uncomfortably. We sat there for 30 minutes, and then the session ended.

I found Wendy in the lobby, reading the latest issue of *People* magazine.

"What the hell?" I said.

"That guy is obviously insane," said Wendy.

"I thought he was helpful."

"You just want to get laid. That guy is not okay."

We picked Zoë up from daycare and drove home without speaking. Zoë tried to tell us about her day, but Wendy turned up the radio. I drummed my fingers against the steering wheel so hard one of my bones popped.

"Why isn't anyone saying anything?" asked Zoë.

"Mommy and Daddy need quiet right now," said Wendy.

Zoë bounced up and down in her booster seat. The seatbelt annoyed her, so she unbuckled it.

"You have to keep your seatbelt buckled," said Wendy.

"It's uncomfortable," said Zoë.

"It's the law. We have to keep you safe."

"I don't feel good."

Zoë made pretend vomiting sounds. When we ignored her, she pulled her hair so hard she started screaming.

Wendy spun around and said, "Stop that this second or no TV for one week!"

"My hair hurts," said Zoë.

"Stop pulling it!" screamed Wendy.

When we got home, Wendy started to put Zoë in timeout, but noticed she had a fever.

"Oh, you poor thing," said Wendy. "You're burning up."

"I don't feel good," said Zoë.

Wendy took Zoë's temperature and started running a bath for her. I fed a blank piece of paper into my typewriter.

"You're not working on your novel, are you?" asked Wendy.

"I'm doing homework," I said.

"On a typewriter?"

"It's for my novel-writing class."

Wendy was silent for a long time, during which I heard her softly weeping.

"Are you actually in a novel-writing class?" she asked.

"Yes?" I said.

"I don't believe you."

"Why can't you just trust me? You never believe a word I say."

Zoë started throwing up in the bathtub. Wendy went to comfort her. I put on a pair of headphones and started working on a new chapter of my book.

I felt terrible for lying, but I really believed I was going to lift my family out of poverty with the power of words.

I was like Wile E. Coyote the moment he runs off the cliff and hovers there for a second in the air. Everything was fine as long as I never looked down.

28

O Captain, My Captain

My plan was to major in accounting or the stock market or whatever it was that rich people majored in so I could make a lot of money, but every time I signed up for classes, I accidentally enrolled in a bunch of writing courses, and two years later, at the time of my graduation, was astonished to discover that I'd earned a bachelor's degree in English.

With a diploma only marginally more useful than no diploma at all, I went to the career counselor and asked for advice.

She said, "How about working as a copywriter?"

I said, "You mean advertising? I'd rather eat my own shit."

She said, "What about a technical writer?"

I said, "I got bored before you even finished that sentence."

She said, "English teacher?"

I thought about it for a second. The idea wasn't completely stupid. I was a failure in everything I'd set out to accomplish in my life, but when I looked back at high school, my best teachers were failures. Life had broken their spirits; without anything to live for, those underachievers told it like it was. "Your parents are bastards," they'd say, sipping black coffee, staring out the window. "The principal is a pedophile. Don't listen to your teachers; they're trying to brainwash you."

Honest to goodness wisdom I wish I'd paid more attention to while I was running around trying to figure out the meaning of life.

"If I did decide to become a teacher," I said, "how would I go about making that happen?"

The guidance counselor explained that Mount Mansfield had a program for graduates like me. All I had to do was submit to a criminal background check and if I passed, they'd hire me.

Other than my false imprisonment by two campus police officers back in 1996, my criminal record was squeaky clean.

Two weeks later I was lecturing a motley gang of 17-year-olds on the use of repetition in Edgar Allan Poe's "The Raven." My students were the seventh-generation offspring of cousin-loving dairy farmers named Dale and Edna. They had wide-set eyes, reeked of alfalfa, and cultivated menacing personalities to offset the wholesomeness of their agrarian lives.

At first, I did a good impersonation of someone who cared about his job. I took roll, assigned homework, and stood in front of the chalkboard, discoursing in a rambling manner that passed for a public education. But after a while my depression took hold. I arrived to class hungover, occasionally still drunk. I forgot my students' names, lost their papers, and developed a grading system based on the Magic 8 Ball and a tattered copy of the *I Ching* since I rarely bothered to read the essays I'd assigned.

One morning I showed up to first period with a coffee stain on my crotch and my hands trembling like scared little birds. My students, typically asleep or burning their knuckle hair with cigarette lighters, looked up from their desks. They seemed genuinely concerned.

"Is everything okay, Mr. Maloney?" asked a boy in the back of the class, wearing a studded leather collar.

"Yeah," I said. "I just—"

I reached for a piece of chalk and noticed that my arms weren't covered in the usual blue cloth of my Oxford dress shirt. I seemed to be wearing a tank top with the Red Hot Chili Peppers logo on it.

"I'm fine," I said. "It's laundry day. Can everyone please stop looking at me like that?"

I wasn't motivated enough to assign a seating chart. Of their own accord, my students segregated themselves into hierarchical power structures. Up front were the feeble-minded do-gooders. They were eager to learn, but something important was missing from their brains. They parroted back to me whatever asinine thing I'd said the day before—"winging it," since I rarely used lesson plans.

In back sat the angry geniuses. They were smarter than me and they knew it. I felt guilty making eye contact with them. They were all flirting with the idea of becoming alcoholics and, therefore, recognized the disease in me. They could have used this against me, but they were too indifferent to engage in something as time-consuming as blackmail. You know the type: Pink Floyd t-shirt, torn jeans, forever drawing beautiful blue knives on the shiny wooden tops of their desks. In a better world, their kind would be revered. We'd worship them as saints. In this world, they were biding their time, waiting for their misdemeanors to turn into felonies, sealing their fates forever.

"What are we reading?" I asked.

"*Of Mice and Men*," said an attentive girl in the front row, who couldn't do basic arithmetic.

I borrowed her copy, turned to page one, and nearly burst into tears. I hate *Of Mice and Men*. I wanted to stand up on my desk like Robin Williams in *Dead Poets Society*, only instead of quoting Robert Frost and Alfred Lord Tennyson, I'd read a few choice lines from Bukowski and blow their minds forever.

But I did as I was told. I read aloud from *Of Mice and Men.* As I read, I slept with my eyes open. I took a beautiful nap. At one point, I dreamed I was a great writer, a million times better than John Steinbeck. I'd written one of those rare books— funny, brilliant, edgy—that cause teenage boys to drop out of high school and hitchhike to Nicaragua, where they spend the rest of their lives writing haiku poetry in a geodesic dome. I pictured my students reading the final pages of my novel, gazing at me in wonder, then standing on top of their desks, the safety pins on their jackets gleaming with fluorescent light.

"Oh Captain, my captain!" they'd say. "Oh Captain, my captain!" One after another until the only ones still seated were the do-gooders who didn't understand the fiery beauty of my deranged mind.

When the afternoon bell rang, I spent an hour pretending to revise my lesson plans while secretly working on my novel. Then it was the 45-minute commute home, stuck in rush-hour traffic, the whole time trying to convince myself that this was all going to work out somehow—I'd be a famous novelist with a dozen bestsellers and a wife who loved me.

29

A Dozen Baby Snakes

Between Wendy's part-time secretarial work and my meager first-year teacher's salary, we barely had enough money to stay alive. At the end of every month, we emptied our pockets and scavenged the futon for enough change to pay for diapers and a carton of cigarettes. We didn't have a financial plan or any sort of budget, but I was convinced that if I could finish a decent draft of my novel, I could secure an advance from a major publishing house and all our problems would go away.

I told Wendy that if she could take Zoë to the park for three or four hours, I was pretty sure we'd become millionaires.

She said, "This isn't so you can work on your pornography book, is it?"

I said, "It's a novel, and yes, I think I'm onto something. The characters, plot, and dialogue are a little weak, but otherwise it's the best work I've done."

For some reason, she agreed. I made a pot of coffee and drank it and made a second pot and drank it and sat down at my typewriter and typed as fast as I could without thinking.

Three hours later, I'd finished a draft of my novel. I couldn't believe it. All those years trying to convince my parents that I shouldn't have to mow the lawn because I was a misunderstood genius and here was proof!

I cracked a beer, lit a cigarette, and reread my manuscript. Almost immediately, it occurred to me that what I'd written wasn't so much a novel as a vivid description of various porn sites I'd visited in the past week. There were three gangbang scenarios, two Russian lesbian trysts, and a leaked celebrity home video. In one scene, a married couple gets in a fight about laundry. She yells at him for ruining her favorite sweater by putting it in the dryer. He accuses her of criticizing him whenever he makes a mistake. Then, out of nowhere, the husband lifts the wife onto the dryer and says, "Can you handle my spin cycle, baby?" He gives her three orgasms, and the chapter ends with her saying, "You can load my washer any time."

I stood up and started laughing so hard I couldn't breathe. Little particles appeared in the air all around me, zooming back and forth like tiny UFOs. I said, "I don't feel right," and a second later my body hit the floor.

There was the sound of keys in the front door, followed by Wendy's voice threatening Zoë that if she asked about a cookie one more time, she'd never have a cookie ever again for the rest of her life. Zoë, the poor thing, had never even considered this a possibility. Just the thought of a life without cookies sent her into hysterics; she started throwing up on the carpet and— judging from the distressed meowing coming from the living room—the cat.

"Kevin!" yelled Wendy. "Kevin, I can't do this anymore! Your turn!"

Her words had edges in them. I felt my self-esteem vanish suddenly and realized the world would have been better off if I'd never been born.

I tried to stand up, but I was experiencing a savage tingling on my left side. Also, as of the last minute or two, my heart had hatched like an egg, releasing a dozen baby snakes made of electricity, whose favorite pastime was slithering satanically through my veins.

"I'm feeling weird," I said from the floor.

"Where are you?" asked Wendy. "Zoë, go find Daddy and tell him I quit being a mommy."

Zoë didn't know what was real. She liked having a mommy. She started another round of throwing up.

I tried to sit up, but someone (God?) sawed my skull open, sprinkled Pop Rocks on my brain, and doused them with Coca-Cola. This triggered a chain reaction of vicious explosions that made my fingers wiggle.

The electric snakes were overjoyed by this mayhem. They all began migrating upward, giving me the sensation that gravity had just won some epic battle with the floor, and I was being pushed, finally, down into the center of the Earth, where I'd be consumed by fire and magma.

When Wendy discovered me, she emitted a sound of profound disappointment. Whatever was left of my self-esteem vaporized completely.

"Are you fucking serious?" she said. "God, you're even worse than your kid. Get up and be a man and get your insane daughter the hell away from me."

"I'm dying," I said. "Call an ambulance."

"You're not dying. Listen, I picked up a tiara for Zoë's Halloween costume. We'll be fine repurposing her Ariel outfit from last year. I mean, she'll freak out and I probably won't win any mother of the year awards, but it's something."

She set her car keys on the counter and sniffed the air. "Have you been smoking in here?"

"I'm shaky and my left arm isn't working," I said. "At first I was thinking stroke, but since the snakes hatched, I'm leaning strongly toward heart attack."

My eyes were closed, but I knew from experience that Wendy's arms were folded savagely over her breasts.

Her silence suggested that she was briefly entertaining the possibility that I was actually in peril, a thought she immediately rejected.

"Fine," she said. "Do whatever the hell you want."

"I want to go to the hospital," I said.

"Go for it. Take all day if you have to. Don't worry about me. I'll be locked in the broom closet, curled up in the fetal position."

I briefly opened my eye, long enough to catch a glimpse of Zoë sitting in the corner, holding her knees and rocking in place.

I managed to stand up, a little adventure that made the molecular gnats swarming me wild with rage.

"Okay," I said. "I'm going to the hospital now."

"Knock yourself out," said Wendy.

"Will you come with me?" I asked.

"This is *your* thing. You go have fun with your little ER visit."

I checked in at the ER desk and told the intake nurse that I was having a massive coronary event and needed bypass surgery immediately.

The nurse took one look at me and asked how old I was.

I said, "I'm 28 and I'm definitely dying."

She asked if I'd done any cocaine today.

I said that I hadn't.

She said, "Don't lie to me."

I said, "I'm not lying."

She handed me a clipboard and said, "Okay then, fill this out and sign here, here, and here."

I sat down on a plastic chair and started filling out the form. I wrote my name and social security number, and then the letters broke apart and ran around the paper like tiny insects that I tried to catch and return to their proper positions.

It was a nasty trick the ER nurse was playing on me, making me, a dying person, wait out here with the non-dying people, who only had pneumonia and lacerations they held shut with bloody towels.

I walked up to the window and complained.

The ER nurse took the form from me and said, "Honey, you haven't finished filling this out."

I said, "I know. I'm dying, and my left arm doesn't work."

She said, "You're left-handed?"

I said, "I'm right-handed, but that's not the point."

She wasn't impressed. She called someone's name. A woman limped to the counter, leaving a trail of blood on the floor.

I returned to my chair and tried to fill out the form, but it was useless. When they asked me to list an emergency contact, I accidentally drew a thunderbolt, and when they inquired if I was allergic to any medications, I started crying.

When the doctor released me, I drove home, excited to tell Wendy I'd only had a panic attack, not a heart attack, and would therefore remain her husband for the foreseeable future. But when I got there, I found a note on the kitchen counter that said:

Feeling angry and stressed. Locked myself in bedroom for the night. Leaving Zoë to fend for herself. Lord of the Flies, etc. She'll be fine, right? Fingers crossed.
—W

Zoë was in the bathtub, wearing a mermaid tail and crooked tiara. The water was flowing over the edges. She held a bath toy, a little dog she'd named Mr. Dog. She was making him talk. Before she noticed me standing in the doorway, Mr. Dog said, "Quit crying! Mommy needs some alone time! Have you seen the corkscrew?"

For the second year in a row Zoë dressed as the Little Mermaid for Halloween. She wanted to be a fairy tyrannosaurus rex, but Wendy and I were too tired from fighting all the time to put together a proper costume.

I led Zoë from house to house, doing everything I could to keep from sobbing. My hands wouldn't stop shaking. The pills the doctor gave me for my panic attacks were supposed to make me feel numb, but I felt crazy. A gust of wind shook the trees, and maple leaves, dipped in blood, scuttled across the sidewalk. I ran around trying to pick them up. It didn't seem fair that anything, even the 11-pointed appendages of the Vermont state tree, had to die.

"Trick or treat!" said Zoë.

"Well, aren't you adorable?" said one of our neighbors. "Let me guess. Are you the Little Mermaid?"

"I was supposed to be a dinosaur, but Mommy got tired and Daddy went to the hospital for nerves."

"Oh dear. Well—you make a lovely mermaid."

"Roar!" said Zoë. "ROOOOOOOOARRRRRRR!!!!"

We made it to a dozen houses before I started having a panic attack. I told Zoë Halloween was cancelled; it was time to go home.

We sat in front of the TV, eating candy. Wendy was at a work event, so I didn't have to be a good parent. I let Zoë eat as much candy as she wanted as long as I got to be the "poison tester," which meant I got all the Reese's Peanut Butter Cups.

Zoë said she wanted to watch a scary movie. I put on *It's the Great Pumpkin, Charlie Brown.*

Zoë said, "This movie is for babies," so I put on *The Texas Chainsaw Massacre.*

Leatherface butchered a bunch of people with a chainsaw for no reason, and Zoë whimpered under the blankets.

"Why is the bad man killing everyone?" she asked.

"I don't know," I said. "I guess he doesn't like people."

Zoë started shaking uncontrollably. I tucked her into bed.

"What if someone comes through the window with a chainsaw and kills me?" asked Zoë.

"That kind of thing hardly ever happens," I said. "You're way more likely to die in a car accident."

"Where's Mom?" cried Zoë. "What if she died in a car accident?"

"She's at a work event. She's fine."

"Mom's dead!" wailed Zoë.

I wanted to work on my novel, but instead I sat on the bed, running my fingers through Zoë's hair, assuring her that everything was fine even though it wasn't. I was getting good at lying.

Eventually Wendy came home. Instead of yelling at me she went straight to bed.

"Is everything okay?" I asked.

"I'm really tired," she said.

"How was the Halloween party?"

"Fine? I don't know. I don't want to talk about it."

"Why not?"

"Please. I'm just really tired. Can we talk in the morning?"

I went outside on the porch and lit a cigarette. Little kids ran around dressed as pirates and fairies and begged strangers for candy. Then they went to bed, and it was just a few teenagers throwing pumpkins into the street and smashing beer bottles by throwing them up into the air and waiting for them to fall back to the earth.

I should have yelled at them to stop. Somebody, probably me, was going to have to clean up that glass tomorrow. Instead, I watched those beer bottles spin through the air like fireworks.

"One one-thousand—" I said. "Two one-thousand. Three one-thou—" *Pop!*

Their explosions and the soft tinkling of scattered glass afterward were the prettiest sounds I'd ever heard.

"More!" I said, lighting another cigarette. "More! More! More!"

30

The Odyssey

On a Saturday in November, I assumed my position on the futon, hoping to pass my day drinking Miller High Life and watching college football, when Wendy reminded me that we had a wedding to attend. It was for one of the instructors at the yoga studio where Wendy worked, a mousy woman named Suzanne.

We sat in the back of the church, watching those lovebirds read their vows like they were the first two people on earth who ever fell in love. At one point, I reached for Wendy's hand and squeezed it, hoping to remind her that we too were just like them once, but she recoiled from my touch like my hand was full of poisonous spiders.

Later, when the 20-somethings were dancing to "Crazy in Love" by Beyoncé, I found myself sitting at the kids' table, performing magic tricks. I pulled a coin out of a pigtailed girl's ear, then executed an illusion that made it look like I had the ability to remove part of my finger and put it back on. The children stared at me like I was a deranged god.

I was about to perform my finale—a real humdinger where I put a napkin over a glass of wine, chant the word "Abracadabra," and make the glass miraculously disappear—but halfway through the trick, I looked up and noticed Wendy slow dancing with her boss, Jim Foster. Wendy's cheek was the little spoon to Jim's neck, and his hand was drifting down her naked back until it found a resting place on my wife's sparkly green bottom.

I pulled the napkin off the wine glass.

"It's still there!" screamed the pigtailed girl.

I knocked the wine over and watched the white tablecloth absorb the bright red liquid.

"You're all going to die one day," I said. "Your parents don't love you and your dreams are shit and there's no such thing as the Easter Bunny."

With that, I got in my car and drove home drunk and woke up in a Pizza Hut parking lot with the yellow sun rising through my shattered windshield.

I had three broken ribs and to this day can't make a fist with my right hand, but I managed to call a buddy of mine who owned an auto body shop, who towed my car before the cops got wind of my wreck.

When I showed up to school Monday, my students were even more alarmed than usual.

"What happened to you?" asked María, one of the angry geniuses in back, who owned at least five Notorious B.I.G. t-shirts.

"I drove into a light fixture," I said.

"Were you drunk?"

"I think so. I can't remember."

My candor surprised them. They started asking me all kinds of questions, things adults had been lying to them about for years.

"Have you ever done drugs?" asked Adam, a long-haired stoner.

"I've smoked my weight in pot," I said. "Mushrooms were amazing. I've Robo-tripped on at least a dozen occasions, but I don't recommend it. It's a dirty high."

"Do you actually read our papers, or do you just grade them randomly?" asked a girl who the *I Ching* had recently given a C-minus.

"The *I Ching* isn't random," I said. "Next."

A virgin asked about sex. The other students laughed, but I told them to shut up. I said that sex is beautiful and holy, and that there's no better feeling in the world than ejaculating inside a woman's pussy, but it has to be the right woman.

"That's the problem with sex," I said. "We're always making love to the wrong people."

The bell rang. I figured word would get around that Mr. Maloney was lecturing his class about Robo-tripping and creampies, so I told the principal I was feeling sick and drove home.

Maybe it was the same day I told those kids about my car accident and the perilous joys of drugs and fucking. Maybe it was a different day. It doesn't matter. It was around this time that I came home from work and found a moving van parked in the street with a Tetris version of our apartment inside. There was the spare futon mattress on top of my IKEA dresser, sandwiched between my writing desk and the gas grill barbecue my dad bought me three years earlier for my birthday. The movers were sitting on the tailgate, smoking cigarettes, joking about some poor bastard who was about to have the worst day of his life.

When they noticed me, a hush came over the group. Suddenly they were ornithologists, gazing up into the tree boughs, trying to identify various species of chickadee and blue jay.

"What's going on?" I asked.

One of the movers took off his baseball hat. "We're just following orders, sir."

"From who?"

"Your wife."

His coworker snorted briefly through his nose.

When I was in college, I read *The Odyssey* by Homer. There's a scene where Odysseus returns to Ithaca in disguise, only to find a gang of drunken suitors harassing his wife. In the mêlée that follows, among other swift deaths delivered by Odysseus, he cuts off one of the suitors' testicles and feeds it to the dogs. I imagined myself doing something like that. Something gruesome. Scrotum-reducing. The problem was I didn't have a sword, just a canvas briefcase with a laptop inside.

"Well, all right then," I said. "Thanks for all your hard work."

Inside, I found Wendy sitting at the kitchen table, holding a mug of tea. Her eyes were red-rimmed, her jaw clenched. It was an expression I hadn't seen in all the years we'd been together: pain mixed with inevitability, like a child about to rip the wings off a butterfly.

I set my briefcase down. Humphrey pushed his head against my leg, then strutted over to the litter box and squatted in the confused, euphoric posture of an excreting pet. I waited for Wendy to make a cutting remark about the smell, to remind me that I never emptied the litter box, but she just sat there staring out the window, repeatedly dunking a teabag into her mug.

"Where's Zoë?" I asked.

"At a friend's," she said.

I waited for her to go on, but she kept sitting there staring out the window.

When she finally spoke, instead of saying hurtful things about my personality, she told me that she loved me. I didn't understand. The sun was setting behind our neighbor's bamboo fence. Half of Wendy's face was orange. Her freckles glowed like campfire embers. She told me what a good man I was, how kind and decent and thoughtful. How happy she was that we'd had a child together. No matter what else happened, she said, we'd always have that.

I noticed that she was wearing makeup. Lip gloss and eye shadow. The eye shadow had sparkles in it. I thought of the time we slow danced to a Merle Haggard song at a cowboy bar in Amarillo, Texas, her big-nosed face made psychedelic by the spinning disco ball. I couldn't remember the last time she'd made any effort to look sexy.

She was struggling to find the right words. She appeared to be in pain. Finally, she said, "I don't want to be married to you anymore."

"Are you serious?" I asked.

She nodded.

"Because of the litter box? Jesus. I'll clean it. I'll clean it right now."

"It's not that. I just—I can't do this anymore."

Her dress was new too. The neckline was lower than her other dresses. She wasn't wearing a bra. I could see blue rivers in her breasts. Veins. I wanted to take those heavenly mounds into my mouth, to sit underneath her and be dizzy with love the way we were in the old days when nothing made sense and we couldn't stop kissing even hours after making love.

"We haven't been happy for a long time," she said.

"I just want to have sex with you. Why don't we have sex anymore?"

"Because I'm not in love with you."

I put my head in my hands and started crying.

"How does every other weekend with Zoë sound?" asked Wendy.

"I don't know," I said. "I can't think about all this stuff right now."

"I'll have my attorney get ahold of your attorney. Oh, you should think about hiring an attorney. The moving guys can take your stuff wherever you want. I reserved a storage unit for you and put it on your credit card. They can drop it off there. Hope you don't mind. I just really felt the need to purge."

I stood up and walked outside. Humphrey snuck out the door and stood next to me.

"I should have cleaned your litter box," I said.

Humphrey flopped onto his side and licked himself.

"I made a big mistake."

The movers rolled down the window. "What's the plan, bud?"

"I'm going to kill myself," I said.

"I mean with your things."

"I don't care. Throw everything in Lake Champlain."

The moving van's engine roared. I watched it turn onto the highway, and then it was quiet except for the occasional chirp of a chickadee in the trees and the deep heave of my childlike sobbing.

PART IV
DARK NIGHT OF THE SOUL

31

Walden Pond

For the next two weeks, I behaved like a man who any minute expected to be invited back home to his wife and child—I lived out of my car, called in sick to work, and drank heavily to maintain the illusion that I was a happily married man on vacation in my own city. At night, I walked up and down Church Street, peering into dimly lit bars where 21-year-old hipsters lounged about, ogling one another. They had no idea what awaited them on the other side of their horniness: insemination, marriage, shit-filled Huggies, insomnia, exhaustion (physical and spiritual), and the gradual disintegration of what they mistook for *true love* because, only two decades out of the womb, they didn't understand yet that life is about taking care of other people. Like a clairvoyant, I watched their stylish lives veer precipitously into the toilet, but I didn't know how to stop them. I could only gape at the slow-motion catastrophe, drunk, through a pane of glass.

There was one bar in particular, a music venue called the Radio Lounge. The patrons were Marxists and aspiring painters—gaunt intellectual types in horn-rimmed glasses and lumberjack costumes, carrying recently purchased copies of *Infinite Jest* under their arms.

One night I found myself drinking Pabst Blue Ribbon in their midst. I felt a thousand years older than them, but I was only 29, and my fashion sense, deeply rooted in grunge culture, had come full circle, allowing me to pass for one of these stylish hipster's jaded older cousin.

I must've been on my sixth or seventh pint when I noticed a young couple sitting nearby. The boy wore a red and black checked flannel and oversized librarian glasses. The girl had a faint mustache and wore an Urban Outfitters shawl. Their fingers were laced together. The girl smiled at everything the boy said. Poor bastard, he didn't know yet that he was only an experiment, a sandbox for this vicious fox to play in until somebody better came along.

I walked over to where they were sitting and plopped down at an empty chair. They ignored me as long as they could, but my unflinching gaze and forceful nasal breathing made them uncomfortable. Finally, the girl asked what I was staring at.

"You're going to destroy that poor lamb," I said, indicating the emaciated librarian sitting on her lap.

"What are you talking about?" she asked.

"He's just a child and you're a woman. It isn't fair."

The boy stood up. "Shut up, mister! You're drunk. Leave my girlfriend alone."

I'd never been less scared. It was like watching a chipmunk try to hold a sword.

I tried to put him at ease. "I'm not saying she should have sex with *me*. I'm even more pitiful than you are. Hell, I don't think there's a guy in this bar who wouldn't be completely shattered by this poisonous flower you seem to be making love to. There probably isn't a man on earth who could handle it. She'll end up a lesbian, the poor thing."

A hush came over the bar. The band appeared to be too uncomfortable to play their instruments. I felt sorry for this generation of talented babies. I decided to do something about it. Standing up on my chair, in the voice of a schoolmaster, I gave them an important lesson: "Enjoy it while it lasts, bitches!"

And then, because they seemed unaware of even the most basic facts: "Are any of you actual tree-cutting professionals? Show of hands. Yeah, that's what I thought. Oh, by the way, your music sucks, Sufjan Stevens is a mouth-breather, and Pearl Jam is the greatest band of all—wait, I'm going to throw up." With that, I filled my hands with soupy vomit that dripped between my fingers.

My little performance caused a commotion. Before I finished wiping my hands on my jeans, a mean fucker in a Modest Mouse t-shirt snatched me from my chair and informed me that I was no longer welcome in this depressing establishment. He directed my attention to the front door, and when I expressed reservations about abandoning my half-finished beer, he kicked me in the balls.

Ever since I read the "Economy" chapter of *Walden* in Mrs. Frisbie's Honors English class, I'd been trying to find ways to reduce my expenses so I could lessen my employment so I could spend my one precious life walking around, enjoying the beauty of Planet Earth. I'd read books on subsistence farming and off-grid geodesic domes, but it was here, in my darkest hour, that I discovered my very own Walden Pond: my 1991 Ford Tempo. It wasn't the idyllic shack in the woods I'd fantasized about in my youth, but the rent was zero, and if you got tired of the view, you just drove it across town and parked somewhere else. The only problem was Wendy. She wouldn't let Zoë spend the night. She had antiquated ideas about what constituted an "apartment" and demanded that I rejoin the unhappy masses, working every second of my life in exchange for an expensive box to sleep in.

Reluctantly, I bid farewell to my vagabond lifestyle and moved into a squalid apartment located directly above the Radio Lounge. All those degenerate artists I'd drunkenly lectured about Pearl Jam and the fleeting nature of happiness became my friends. The girl with the mustache's name was Penelope. When I told her and her librarian boyfriend about my wife leaving me, they saw me less as a piece of shit and more as a pathetic bastard with a drinking problem—the same as them.

The bouncer who kicked me in the balls became my best friend. His name was Frank. His wife had left him too. Every night at Happy Hour, we met at the back tables of the Radio Lounge and drowned our sorrows while bedazzled children, barely older than Zoë, played Velvet Underground covers on Fender Stratocasters their parents bought them six months ago.

"This is going to sound shallow," said Frank, shaking his head. "But my ex-wife had this way of shaving her pubic hair—completely bare except for this stripe on top. It drove me crazy. Usually I'm confident around women, but with her, I was a fucking baby. She could tell me to do anything—it didn't matter what—and I'd do it. It doesn't feel good, being in love like that. It feels like dying. I didn't know who I was anymore. Toward the end, when she cheated on me, it made me question my entire existence. Like, how can I trust myself? It's been six months, and I still feel completely lost."

I nodded. "The first time I met Wendy, I was dressed like a semi-retired large animal veterinarian. She gave me directions to a bar. I almost lost my virginity to these two girls, Sarah and Yvonne, but I screwed up and lost my virginity to Wendy instead."

I'd meant the story to sound romantic, but it sounded stupid. Frank didn't judge me though. He went to the bar and bought us another round. We toasted to a lifetime of being crushed, spiritually, by ever more beautiful women.

32

Team Daddy

At first Zoë was excited by my new apartment. Lacking things like chairs and bowls, we found ourselves eating cereal directly from the box while reclining on my futon, watching *The Simpsons* on illegal streaming websites. I didn't know how to cook, so I bought food with cartoon characters on the packaging: Barbie Pop Tarts, Shrek 2 Go-Gurt, Scooby-Doo Mini Pizza Breadsticks. We gobbled up those neon snacks, then lay on the floor for hours in protracted sugar comas.

Our official explanation to Zoë re: our separation was that Mommy and Daddy needed a "timeout" to sort out our differences. But after six months of sorting (roughly 11 percent of Zoë's life), our little genius did some math and figured out that whatever weird vacation Daddy was on wasn't so much a vacation as a downward spiral into slovenliness and depression.

One day when I picked Zoë up from daycare, she refused to speak to me. I tried to trick her into talking by pretending that

I was dead, and when that didn't work, that our apartment was on fire, but she was a shrewd little monkey, much smarter than I gave her credit for.

Finally, I bribed her with an ice cream cone. Between licks, she finally asked the question she'd been pondering for weeks in silence: "Am I going to have two daddies now like Willem?"

"Of course not," I laughed. "I'm not gay."

"Are you sure?" she asked.

It was a good question. I didn't know what I was. If it turned out I was gay, that would certainly explain a lot of things.

"Listen," I said. "If I find out I'm gay, I promise you'll be the first person I tell."

This satisfied her immensely, as did the cookie dough monstrosity I'd bribed her with, hoping in this way to convince her that Team Daddy was better than Team Mommy.

Zoë stayed with me every other weekend from Friday afternoon until Sunday evening. I didn't know what to do with a 4-year-old, so I took her to Border's and bought her books she was too young to understand—*Catch-22*, *The Stranger*, and *Slaughterhouse-Five*. Then we found our way to one of Burlington's "family friendly" bars that allowed minors until 8 p.m.

"What's *lousy*?" asked Zoë.

"It's an old-fashioned way of saying *sucks*," I said, taking a sip of beer.

"Who's David Copperfield?" she asked.

"I don't know. A magician? Like the guy with the long white beard in *Harry Potter*."

Zoë nodded and kept reading, her face buried in the iconic red cover of *The Catcher in the Rye*.

"What's *crap*?" she asked.

"It's a bad word," I said. "But not that bad... like *poop* or *turd*."

"Crap," she said.

"You got it."

"Crap!" she said again, only louder.

"Home run."

The waitress came by and asked if I wanted another beer. I said sure.

"That's some heady reading there, young lady," said the waitress, nodding to Zoë. "Sure you understand all those big words?"

Zoë scowled and knocked over her water on purpose. The waitress had to clean it up. I tried not to laugh, but I couldn't help it. Everything was so incredibly fucked up that I'd become completely indifferent to the consequences of my actions.

The waitress brought me another IPA. I took a long sip and felt all my problems turn into a blurry rainbow.

Zoë asked why I liked beer so much.

I pushed my glass over to her.

She took a sip and made a disgusted face.

"Yeah," I said. "I didn't like it when I was your age either."

We sat there for a while in silence. Zoë gave up trying to read *The Catcher in the Rye*. I moved my fingernail back and forth along the sticky tabletop. Finally, I said, "—unless your mom gets remarried."

Zoë gave me a confused look.

"You might have two dads if your mom gets remarried."

When we got home, I didn't feel like being a parent, so I put on *The Simpsons*. Zoë watched three episodes in a row, and then my computer got a virus from looking at porn all the time, and naked women appeared all over the screen.

Zoë started screaming, so I gave her a bottle of ketchup and a grocery bag and pretended it was art supplies. She painted for a while, then complained that my art supplies were just food and a bag. She said last week Mommy bought her a 64-pack of

Crayola markers and a 12" x 18" drawing pad. Apparently while I was depressed and not paying attention, Wendy had made a huge leap forward in the parental Cold War, becoming the "cool" parent, while I was the lazy one who pretended ketchup was paint.

I drove Zoë to the art store and bought her a 128-pack of colored markers and an 18" x 24" drawing pad. We spent the rest of the night making art. Zoë drew a tyrannosaurus rex named DADDY who ate Care Bears and My Little Ponies and otherwise ruined all the happy things in the world. I drew a picture of a woman with freckles and pretty red lips crying because of all the bad decisions she'd made in her life.

Zoë looked at my drawing and said, "Why is Mommy crying?"

"It's not Mommy," I said.

"Yes, it is."

"No. It's just some lady."

Zoë leaned over, and with the brightest red in the 128-marker set, wrote: SHES CRYING BECUSE YOUR STUPID.

33

Head & Shoulders

One night when I dropped Zoë off at Wendy's apartment, Wendy said there was something we needed to talk about. We went outside and sat on wet lawn furniture. There were toys scattered everywhere—Care Bears without arms, tricycles without wheels, and some kind of play structure from an era when parents didn't worry about jagged edges. I rolled a cigarette. Wendy lit an American Spirit.

I tried to be mad at her for ruining my life, but every time I gave her a nasty look, it accidentally turned into a smile. Wendy was too pretty to be mean to. The wide neck of her t-shirt hung down over a freckled shoulder, revealing a green bra strap. Her jeans were a designer brand—something expensive where you poured your legs in and the jeans contoured your jiggling fat into voluptuous curves.

"I'm concerned about your alcoholism," said Wendy.

"I'm not an alcoholic," I lied.

"Zoë said most of the time you're together you take her to bars. She knows what a *beer back* is. I'm concerned."

I gazed out at the yard and noticed one of Zoë's shoes in a vegetable patch. There was a weed growing out of it. The garden we worked on so hard last year was a depressing graveyard of moldy tomato vines.

"I'm having a hard time," I admitted. "I miss being a family."

"It's better this way," said Wendy.

"I keep telling myself that, but I don't think it's true."

I started crying. Wendy put her arm around me and held me as I slobbered onto her shirt.

"There's something I want to show you," she said. "Follow me."

She led me to her bedroom, which used to be our bedroom. I sat on the bed, which was just a mattress on the floor covered in afghans. She said she'd be right back and disappeared into the bathroom.

There was a night, maybe a month or two after we started dating, when we sat on the floor of my bedroom, listening to Leonard Cohen's *Songs of Love and Hate*. Our conversation came to a lull, and by accident, without realizing what I was doing, I said, "I love you." Wendy said, "I love you too." We started laughing and then kissing, and then we were on the mattress on the floor, moving in slow circles, panting. The look on Wendy's face scared me. I thought I was hurting her, but then she cried out in happiness and clung to me like if she let go, she'd fall forever. Afterward we discovered that the condom had come off inside of her and that she was full of my semen. I kissed her over and over as she whispered, "Fuck, fuck, fuck, fuck," sitting on a towel, trying to get my cum to drip out of her.

She wasn't pregnant that time, but two years later she was.

Wendy stepped out of the bathroom, holding a bottle of Head & Shoulders. "Here," she said.

I took the bottle from her and looked at it, trying to understand its meaning.

"I noticed when you were crying that your dandruff is back," she said.

"Oh. Okay. Thank you."

"Um yeah, so I should probably tell you. Remember how we promised we'd tell each other if anything happened with somebody else? Well, I've started seeing someone. Actually, it's my boss, Jim. He goes by Ashram now. He sold his yoga studio and started a chiropractic clinic. Well, more of a healing and wellness center. Body work. Crystals. That kind of thing. Anyhow, you might start seeing him around. He sort of lives here now. He's at a workshop thing in Scottsdale, but he'll be back Tuesday."

I didn't understand. Like any emotionally stunted 29-year-old, I'd assumed that by recalling our experiences of shared trauma, I'd gain enough emotional capital to initiate some form of sex with Wendy, if not resume our marriage exactly where we left off, only without any problems.

Following a sexual momentum completely at odds with Wendy's announcement, I started taking off my pants.

"What are you doing?" she asked.

"I want to be inside of you," I said.

"What? No! Stop. You need to leave. There's something wrong with you."

I put my pants back on. She led me to the front door. I tried waving to Zoë as I passed the living room, but *Dora the Explorer* had bewitched her by revealing the contents of her backpack, which included a map of the rainforest and a wooden flute.

"Oh, one more thing," said Wendy. "I was talking to my attorney. He's kind of a big deal. He usually only works for celebrities, but he's agreed to represent me in our divorce proceedings. Anyway, I've filed a motion seeking full custody. If you haven't hired a lawyer yet, you should get on that ASAP."

"I still get Zoë every other weekend, right?" I said.

"Well, no," said Wendy. "Not if I win. To be honest, I'm not sure you're in a healthy place right now."

She handed me a pile of divorce papers and pushed me out the door. I took a few steps and sat down on the sidewalk. I felt dizzy. Whatever this world was with its stupid oceans and annoying mountains, I didn't want to be a part of it anymore. Love hurt too much. It wasn't worth it. Even breathing struck me as a laborious imposition I was anxious to be done with once and for all.

I popped the cap of the shampoo, and in bright blue cursive letters, wrote on the concrete: "I DON'T LOVE YOU ANYMORE!!!"

I reread what I wrote and added the word "STUPID" at the end.

I read it one more time and added, "UNLESS YOU CHANGE YOUR MIND, IN WHICH CASE I'M OPEN TO TALKING ABOUT IT ☺"

When I got home from Wendy's, Frank was sitting on the front steps of my apartment building, wearing a cowboy hat and jean shorts, absentmindedly strumming a ukulele.

"There you are!" he said. "I've been looking all over for you."

"I'm in a really bad mood," I said.

"Perfect. I have just the thing for that."

He followed me upstairs.

I went to the bathroom and put the dandruff shampoo in the shower because I actually needed some shampoo, and then I started sobbing.

"What's wrong?" asked Frank.

"Wendy's dating someone," I said.

"Fuck."

"This guy with high body temperature. His name used to be Jim, but he changed it to Ashtray. I think she might have been sleeping with him before we broke up."

"Dang."

"I'm going to kill myself."

"I bet you wish you could just wave a magic wand and make all the painful feelings go away."

He held a baggie in the air. It was full of golden-brown rocks.

"Opium," he said. "I got it from my buddy Antoine. It gives you good dreams, even when you're wide awake."

I said I wasn't into hard drugs.

He said, "What does it matter if you're going to kill yourself?"

He had a point.

We burned that beautiful brown sludge and felt our blood turn into heavenly rivers. Then we smoked an eighth ounce of weed and shared a 40 of Olde English and watched a movie called *The Holy Mountain* on VHS that to this day keeps me up at night, haunting my sleep. What I'm saying is, we got fucked up in a royal manner I wasn't accustomed to, and at some point, the world switched off, and when it switched back on again, I was lying on my floor covered in the half-digested relics of a microwave pizza. There was vomit in my eye sockets, and when I stood up, tomato soup poured out of my navel and soaked my underwear.

I stumbled to the bathroom and took a shower in my clothes and stepped out and looked at myself in the mirror. I looked dead. Beyond dead. I looked like I'd traveled to the underworld and come back—not for religious purposes, but to provide an example to thrill-seeking teenagers to get their shit together.

"Frank!" I called out. "Hey, Frank! What did you do to us? I look like a ghoul!"

Frank was gone. Probably he'd run off somewhere and died too. We'd make a lovely pair of zombies in the morning.

I stripped off my wet clothes and searched my apartment for something clean to wear, but I hadn't done laundry in six months. Most of my shirts had mold spores growing on them. A Black Sabbath concert t-shirt I bought at Value Village in the late '90s had become the dwelling place for a family of spiders.

Rooting around in my closet, I came upon a Hefty bag full of clothes I hadn't opened since moving into my new apartment. It was mostly socks and boxer shorts, but at the very bottom, I uncovered a sparkling green cocktail dress—one of Wendy's I must have grabbed by accident the day I came home to a moving van in the driveway.

Without thinking about it, I put on the dress and walked outside. There was a crowd of people standing in front of the Radio Lounge. It was 11 p.m. The band was taking a break, and everyone had filed outside to smoke cigarettes.

I walked up to the crowd and bummed an American Spirit from a woman I knew.

Actually, you know her too—it was Penelope.

"Look at you!" she said.

"Look at what?" I asked.

"You're wearing a dress. You look hot."

I looked down. Did I look hot? I looked like a guy who didn't have clean clothes, who spent his free time smoking opium and eating Shrek 2 Go-Gurt.

I wasn't a barbarian. I didn't want to squeeze in on some dork librarian's girlfriend, but I happened to know that Penelope had recently broken things off with her withered book lender, who'd been so brokenhearted he'd moved back to whatever Midwestern town he'd sojourned here from, seeking his one true love.

Penelope and I sat at an outdoor table. I ordered us a round. She said, "You need makeup."

I said, "Fine. Go crazy."

She pulled a tube of lipstick out of her purse and started painting my face. I don't know whether it made me look ridiculous or beautiful. I didn't care. Penelope sensed my indifference and immediately fell in love with me. I should have been happy.

She was leaning over me, touching me, laughing at my jokes. But a deep hatred of life had penetrated me, and I didn't trust anyone.

I had three drinks, which normally would have given me a pleasant buzz, but I'd been high on opium a few hours earlier, and the alcohol made me sober. Penelope and I went upstairs and fooled around a little, but it didn't amount to much. Something in my heart was sick. I just wanted to listen to music.

I put on a Joy Division record. Penelope had never heard of them. I told her all about Ian Curtis, how he used to dance on stage like he'd been stung by a hornet, and how he suffered from epilepsy like Fyodor Dostoyevsky, and how he committed suicide one night by hanging himself, but first he watched Werner Herzog's *Stroszek* and listened to Iggy Pop's *The Idiot*.

Before you get all high and mighty, I know what you're thinking, and you're right. I was mansplaining. I was the worst kind of bastard, dropping facts about art on a young woman so she'd see me as an authority figure and look up to me. All of that's true. But I didn't have any self-esteem, and suddenly I felt important, talking about this world I used to care about so much and that I'd lost track of, and which suddenly felt vital to me, as if my continued existence depended on it.

That night, Penelope and I shared a bed. We fell asleep holding each other, and when I woke up in the middle of the night and kissed her neck, she tasted different than Wendy.

I wasn't in love with her, but it was a kind of miracle, sleeping with my arms wrapped around another woman. I saw that this world was big and that anything was possible, and that no matter how bad it gets, there are always my dead heroes in their graves not making art anymore, inspiring me to use what little time I have.

34

Fur-Bassador

Wendy's lawyer was a shark. A few days later, I got a letter in the mail demanding that I be in court on such-and-such date, or I'd lose all custodial rights to my daughter. The letter inquired whether I'd obtained the services of an attorney so he could share the evidence he planned on using against me, which among a bunch of legal mumbo jumbo included reference to an exhibit they'd usefully titled "Email #4—6/10/2006."

I logged into my Yahoo account and looked in my "Sent" folder. Sure enough, there was an e-mail addressed to Wendy that I didn't remember sending:

Dear Beyotch,

I don't love you!!! Shit. That's not true. I love you so much. Wow. Like, a lot. Should we have more babies????????????????? Oh wait, you don't love me anymore. Forgot. Dang, I'm drunk. Also stoned? Remember pot? I bought some!!!! My field of vision keeps going whack-whack-whack to the left every time my heart beats. Does yours go left too? Does everybody's? Hey got an

idea. Send me a picture of your pussy. Also tits, but not as impor-
tant. Do you still love me as much as I love you??????????????
Oh wait you don't! That's so dumb. I want a time machine. I want
to go back to when you loved me, when your brain was different.
Except I don't want to go back so far our kid disappears. You
know who I mean. What's her name? Why can't I remember her
name? Did I go to the past? Oh fuck. Wait—lemme. Zoë. Ha.
Got it. YES!!! Wait, why did we name her that? Did we really put
two dots over our kid's name? What's she gonna do in school?
Everybody's gonna make fun of her. Wasn't that name your idea?
Hey did you send me that pussy pic? Lemme check. You did!!!!!
Oh wait, no that's an email from my mom. I hope she didn't send
me a pussy pic. That'd be weird. I don't want to see my m

The email ended there, quite mysteriously. I couldn't stop
laughing. That email was amazing. Except that Wendy's lawyer
was going to read it out loud in a courtroom right before the
judge decided whether or not I got to see my kid every other
weekend from now until she went to college.

I was feeling pretty pissed, so I sent Wendy an e-mail that
said:

WTF you seriously printed out that email and gave it to your
lawyer what part of PRIVATE don't you understand are you
a Nazi??? I hate you. All time worst people:

1. Wendy
2. Hitler
3. I don't fucking care

I pressed send. A few minutes later, I got a new email in my
inbox. It was from Wendy's lawyer, Monty Gilbreath. He said
that any e-mails I sent to Wendy were automatically forwarded
to him and entered as evidence in our case.

"You would do well to refrain from any future contact with Wendy," he suggested. "Then again, I'm not your attorney, and to be honest, you're really helping our case, so now that I think about it, feel free to keep them coming. —Monty"

I was feeling scared and helpless, so I googled, "Best divorce lawyers in Burlington, Vermont." All the results came up with the same name: Monty Gilbreath. Most of the websites I consulted disagreed about who was second best, so I picked one at random and called it.

The receptionist said, "Thanks for calling the law offices of Smith and Buleri. How can I help you?"

I said, "My wife and I separated recently and there's a good chance we'll get back together so this call probably isn't necessary, but apparently she hired an attorney and he's threatening to take my kid away and I guess there are some pretty disgusting e-mails which I seemed to have written when I was drunk and high, but like I said I'm sure it's nothing."

The receptionist taught me a little breathing exercise, which I did so I could calm down enough to have a conversation.

"We'd be happy to help," she said. "You mentioned your wife retained the services of a lawyer. Do you mind me asking who?"

"Monty Gilbreath," I said.

"Oh wow. He's good."

I told her that I needed some pretty serious legal advice. I wanted their best lawyer. *Numero uno.*

She said, "No problem. Our most experienced divorce attorney is Leah Buleri, one of the firm's partners."

"Perfect," I said. "How much does she cost?"

"Your initial consultation is free, but if you decide to retain our firm, Ms. Buleri's billing rate is $350 per hour."

I just so happened to know that I had exactly 73 cents in my bank account. I had to use the shit out of my free consultation.

The receptionist put me through to Ms. Buleri. She spoke incredibly fast. Her words had freakish precision, like you'd expect of someone whose time was worth 10 cents a second. I gave her a very brief overview of my situation, which she interrupted frequently when I mentioned things like Wendy's breach of contract with God and how I was emotionally distressed from lack of sex.

Ms. Buleri said those weren't actual legal issues and asked if I was wildly rich.

I said no.

"Combined assets?" she asked.

"I have a 1991 Ford Tempo that hasn't had an oil change in 14,000 miles."

"House?"

"No."

"Trust fund?"

"Jesus, I wish."

"Cash on hand?"

"73 cents."

Ms. Buleri explained that hiring her to defend me was like asking Bill Gates to repair a sticky keyboard. She recommended mediation. I tried to protest, but she said she had a Boston Celtic on line two and hung up.

I called Wendy and said, "I give up. You win."

She said, "Already?"

I said, "Divorce is too stressful. Can I please just see Zoë every once in a while?"

She said, "I really wanted to hear those e-mails read in court."

I said, "Can't we work something out?"

She said, "Maybe. Let me think about it."

I was feeling depressed and suicidal, so I went downstairs to the Radio Lounge and drank five beers in rapid succession. The alcohol didn't make my problems go away, but it caused certain endorphins to flood my brain, giving me the sensation that my life was on track, everything A-OK.

When I tried to settle my tab, the bartender said my credit card was declined. I did some math and figured out that I hadn't been to work in six weeks and was almost certainly fired.

"Hey, Carl," I said.

"What's up?" he asked.

"You know how I'm going to be a famous writer one day?"

He shrugged. Everybody in the Radio Lounge was going to be famous one day. Or at least we assumed we were, even though we sat around all day getting drunk, not making art.

"This is going to be worth a lot of money," I said, signing my name on the back of a napkin. "Just don't put it on eBay until I get my novel published."

Before he could protest, I darted out of the bar and ran smack into a line of hipsters that flowed down the sidewalk, around the corner, and ended at a sign with a cartoon bear head on it.

"What's this about?" I asked.

"We're waiting for the Bear Bus," said a guy I sort of knew, an alcoholic sculptor named Pat.

"What's that?"

He explained that not all artists had trust funds; some of them had jobs. Since most of them had dropped out of college in order to zigzag back and forth across the country *burning for the ancient heavenly connection to the starry dynamo in the machinery of night*, they weren't qualified for any sort of work other than sewing teddy bear arms to teddy bear bodies at the Green Mountain Teddy Bear Factory.

"The bus comes every day at noon to pick us up," he said. "If you need some money, get on."

I said that I did need money, but I was drunk.

He said, "It's a teddy bear factory. They don't do drug testing. Can you imagine assembling a teddy bear sober?"

I got on the bus and found a window seat. We zoomed through pastoral landscapes full of black-and-white dairy cows and came to a stop in front of a factory with an enormous brick chimney belching smoke from all those ovens where they cooked teddy bear fur all day.

I followed the line of artists to a gymnasium where you filled out a questionnaire to help figure out which part of the teddy bear factory you were most qualified for. There was only one question:

ARE YOU SCARED OF LOUD NOISES? ☐ *YES* ☐ *NO.*

I checked yes, and a woman in a sweater made of teddy bear fur appeared and said I was being assigned to the call center. She led me to a windowless warehouse behind the windowless factory where bohemians in headsets sat in front of ancient computers, asking customers whether they wanted coffee or buttercream fur on their limited-edition HipHop Bear™.

The woman assigned me to a computer, gave me a five-minute tutorial on how to answer the phone, and disappeared. I wasn't a hundred percent clear what my job responsibilities were, but a second later the phone rang.

"Is this the Teddy Bear Museum?" asked an old woman.

"Um. Something like that," I said.

"I bought a Pilgrim Bear from you people back in November and the arm just fell off. My granddaughter won't stop crying. I told her William Brad-fur just has a booboo, but can you imagine the distress this is causing? Is this the kind of shoddy craftsmanship you folks churn out in New Hampshire?"

There was so much happening I could barely understand it.

"Listen," I said. "I'm so sorry about your bear. Here's what I'm going to do. I'm going to send you an address label. All you have to do is put old Will in a box and slap the label on it and ship it to us and we'll fix him right up. As an apology for your granddaughter's trauma, we're going to offer you a $25 credit off your next order."

The woman was elated. She placed an order for a $499 Jumbo Bear using her new gift credit.

I hung up, sweating, almost certain I was having some kind of flashback from one of my psychedelic drug experiences.

A second later, a man in a suit made of teddy bear fur appeared and told me to follow him. He led me to a back room and asked me to sit down on a sofa upholstered in teddy bear fur.

"That was an incredible call," he said.

"You were listening?" I asked.

"Of course. We monitor every call that comes into the Teddy Bear Factory. That call, young man, was fur-nominal. The best I've heard in months. How would you like to be a manager here? The pay isn't great, and we don't have a health care plan, but every year you get a Bear Bonus. Any bear of your choice, as long as the retail value doesn't exceed $199."

I didn't have any better prospects for employment, so I said sure.

He made me sign an NDA promising I wouldn't sell any bear secrets to Hasbro or Build-A-Bear, then gifted me a Russian fur cap with protruding bear ears and said that for the rest of my life, I would belong to a secret society of teddy bear professionals known as "Fur-bassadors."

I checked my tongue to make sure there wasn't any LSD on it, thanked the man for the promotion, and went back to work.

35

Is This Lunch?

Wendy left a message on my answering machine that said: "Hey! I need a babysitter so Ashram and I can go on a date, and I don't have to pay you, so I've decided you can see your daughter, but only when there's a movie I want to see. Ashram's got a hair up his ass about this new *Mission: Impossible* movie. Will you come over?"

It wasn't the divorce arrangement I was hoping for, but it was something. I said okay.

Wendy opened the door looking healthy and radiant. She said she'd recently taken up yoga and meditation and was strongly considering changing her name to Phoenix.

"You look amazing," I said.

"Thanks," she said. "You look… are you okay?"

I told her I'd gotten a job at a teddy bear factory and that the fur got into my hair and skin and that no amount of washing got it out.

Wendy said there was something we needed to talk about. We went outside and lit cigarettes.

She said, "Oh by the way I quit smoking. This one doesn't count."

I said, "I won't record it in the logbook."

She said, "Smoking's a vestige of my unhappy life with you. As soon as I become Phoenix, I won't put any toxins in my body."

I said, "Congratulations," and took a deep drag and looked up into the sky and watched a 747 fly into a puffy white cloud.

She said, "Here's the deal. Ashram and I are moving to Hawaii. We're taking Zoë with us."

I'd never seriously considered murdering anyone, but Wendy always had a way of introducing me to parts of myself I never knew existed.

I put a cigarette in my mouth only to discover that I already had a cigarette in my mouth. I lit it anyway and took a deep puff and calmly reminded Wendy that I hadn't signed our divorce agreement yet, and that until I did, she wasn't allowed to take Zoë out of the state.

Wendy asked if I was going to play it like that.

I said, "Play it like what?"

She said, "Ashram has a trust fund, so legal costs aren't a problem. We're prepared to bring up the issue of your alcoholism if you make this difficult."

I started coughing, threw up a little, and lit a third cigarette. I'd never hated anyone in my life as much as I hated this woman. I wanted her to be my wife again.

I said, "Okay."

She said, "Really?"

I said, "I fucking hate you."

She said, "I can understand that."

Zoë put on her ladybug boots and *Dora the Explorer* backpack. As we were walking out the door, Wendy said, "Remember to feed her."

I had a pretty strong reaction to that statement, but all the divorce books stressed how important it was not to call your ex-wife a rotten bitch in front of your kid, so I said, "Isn't your mom great? She's the best mom in the world."

Zoë nodded enthusiastically.

We drove past two yoga studios and a maple syrup factory, and then we were in downtown Burlington at a stoplight next to a magnificent church with stained glass windows depicting saints in various acts of sacrifice. Limousines were parked along the curb. Women in matching periwinkle dresses stepped out and hugged each other, and a woman in a wedding dress appeared and the maids of honor lifted her long white train to make sure it didn't get dirty. The bride's hair was flaxen and haloed in purple crocuses.

Zoë said, "Guess who I am."

I said, "I think I'm still in love with your mother."

She made a face and said, "No. Guess who I am."

I said, "Zoë."

She said, "I'm an animal."

I said, "Human."

She shook her head like I was being ridiculous.

I said, "Goat."

She said, "No."

I said, "I have a really bad headache. Can we be quiet for a while?"

I took Zoë to the library and read Dr. Seuss books to her. We made it through *Horton Hears a Who!* and *The Sneetches*, and then I told her to go play with the other kids because I had to go to the bathroom. I sat on the toilet and had explosive diarrhea. When I looked into the toilet, there was blood in it. I didn't have health insurance.

I forgot to feed Zoë until 5 p.m. I took her to the pizza parlor and bought her a slice of cheese pizza.

She asked, "Is this lunch?"

I said, "Yeah, this is lunch."

36

Jeffrey Dahmer

An entitled, cocksure wellness professional with an overzealous body thermometer had supplanted my role as patriarch, but it was fine. Barley, when mixed with hot water and fermented, produced a golden ambrosia that made me feel giddy for a few hours until I threw up.

I went to the Radio Lounge and ordered a Pabst Blue Ribbon.

Carl said, "You have to pay first."

I said, "Since when?"

He said, "I tried to sell your autograph on eBay, but nobody wanted it."

I said, "You have to wait until my novel comes out."

He said, "When's it coming out?"

I said, "I have to write it first!"

I handed him my debit card, hoping one of my relatives had died and direct deposited their will into my bank account, but everybody was alive. The card came back declined. I walked outside, boarded the Bear Bus, and went to work.

It must have been the Fourth of July or close to it. We'd had a rush on our Founding Father Bear, but there was a problem. Jefferson's wig was only attached by a single thread. To undiscriminating golden retrievers across America, that hairpiece must have resembled a delicious snack, because the phone was ringing off the hook with calls from distressed dog owners holed up in vet clinics, waiting to see if Bingo shit out that puffy white toupee or if the doctors had to cut his stomach open and root it out with surgical tools.

"He's being operated on right now!" cried a woman on Line 3. "He might die!"

"I'm so sorry to hear that," I said. "What's your order number?"

"The wig was barely attached. We're going to sue you rotten snow-eaters!"

"This is the first I'm hearing about any wig problem," I lied. "Here's what I'm going to do for you. We're going to send you a Man's Best Friend Bear. And while we're at it, we'll throw in a Get Well Soon Bear. If you give me your order number, I'd be happy to—"

The woman hung up. This wig situation was bigger than free bears and everybody knew it, but the higher ups were trying to avoid litigation with a bonanza of fur giveaways.

On my lunch break I went outside for a cigarette. It was just me and an older lady covered in bear fur—a veteran from the factory floor.

"This wig thing is killing us," I said, taking a drag.

"I told them one stitch wasn't enough," she said.

"I'm offering three… four bears. They just say, 'Talk to my lawyer.'"

"It's like the Can't Help Falling in Love Bear debacle in '03. Elvis's sunglasses shattered into a million X-Acto blades. Fifty people were seriously injured. A 7-year-old girl lost her nose."

I finished my cigarette and lit another. The woman introduced herself. Her name was Gloria. She'd been working at the Green Mountain Teddy Bear Factory for 20 years. In that time, she'd seen a dozen recalls.

"These things have a way of blowing over," she said. "People need bears. Men buy a Cupid Bear for their mistress, and when they get caught, an I'm Sorry Bear for their wife. We'll never go out of business."

All this infidelity talk put me in a sullen mood. Gloria noticed and asked what was wrong.

I told her about my marriage and separation and how even though Wendy was objectively the worst person I'd ever met, I was still in love with her.

Gloria said, "Your wife didn't have sex with you for how long?"

I said, "Two years."

She said, "And you want her back why?"

It was a good question. I hadn't really thought about it.

Gloria stepped into the light. The fur had permanently penetrated her skin. She looked like a werewolf.

"There are a lot of women in this world," she said. "Try not to get hung up on the ones who won't fuck you."

Gloria was right. I needed to stop orienting my life and identity around my ex-wife's every thought and whim. I decided to drive over to Wendy's place and tell her about it.

When I got there, Wendy was sitting on the front porch, crying. She said she and Ashram got in a huge fight and weren't moving to Hawaii anymore. Then she cried so hard she couldn't breathe.

I gave her a hug and kissed her neck and put my hand on her stomach. I kissed her cheeks and her forehead and then I put my tongue in her mouth.

She pulled away and asked what I was doing.

I said I didn't know.

She said I wasn't allowed to do that anymore.

I said sorry.

She said she felt extremely violated.

I said, "I didn't mean to violate you, it just happened."

Zoë opened the back door and said, "Who got violated?"

"Nobody," I said.

"Mommy did," said Wendy. "Daddy violated me."

"No, I didn't," I said. "Don't say that."

Wendy shrugged and lit another cigarette. "As long as you're here, can you watch Zoë for a couple hours? I want to see *The Devil Wears Prada*."

Zoë stole a box of cookies and hopped in my car. We drove downtown. I wasn't hung over, so I remembered to feed her lunch. I ate a burrito, and she had a quesadilla with a dollop of sour cream the size of a golf ball.

She asked if we could have dessert.

I said no.

She started crying.

I felt guilty for being an alcoholic, so we went to Ben & Jerry's and bought double-scoop ice cream cones.

She ate hers so fast she went insane. She ran outside and climbed a statue of a cow, and when I told her to come down, she spit on me.

I said, "That's it. No more ice cream ever!"

She screamed, and a bunch of mothers with well-behaved children shook their heads in judgment.

I yanked Zoë off the statue. She cried and said her arm was broken. One of the judgmental mothers came over and said she saw what happened and was going to report me for child abuse. She asked what my name was.

I said, "Jeffrey Dahmer."

She asked how to spell it.

I said, "F-U-C-K-Y-O-U."

She said, "Stay here," and went to get the police.

I scooped up Zoë and ran as fast as I could. A few blocks away, I set her down in the bark dust at the edge of a parking lot.

I said, "Is your arm really broken?"

She rubbed it and said, "Maybe."

I said, "I'm sorry I pulled you off the statue. I was afraid you'd fall and hurt yourself. I love you."

Instead of saying, "I love you too," she picked up a piece of bark dust and drew a picture on the sidewalk. It was a person with X's for eyes.

I said, "Who's that?"

She said, "You."

I said, "Why are my eyes X's?"

She said, "You're dead."

I picked up a piece of bark dust and tried to draw with her, but it broke in half, so we went to the toy store and bought sidewalk chalk.

We found an expanse of cement in front of American Apparel and drew a huge mural. Zoë drew puppies whose best friends were cats. I illustrated the crucifixion of Jesus Christ. Other kids tugged on their mom's sleeves and asked if they could join us, and suddenly we were in the middle of a mob of children drawing crazy, inspired images that should have been in a museum somewhere but were slowly being trampled by malnourished indie girls walking in and out of American Apparel.

37

Perfect Melody

The next time I saw Wendy her name was Phoenix. She said she and Ashram made up and Hawaii was happening again. Then she said she heard a rumor I was into crossdressing while high on opium.

I said that was none of her business.

She asked if I had any idea what happened to her green cocktail dress.

I said it was possible I'd taken it by accident and worn it on a few occasions, and that I'd be happy to return it if she needed it, as long as she gave it back.

She said, "So you stole it?"

I said, "I took it by accident."

She asked if I could speak a little closer to the microphone.

I said, "What microphone?"

She pointed to a small microphone that she'd placed in the soil of a potted plant on the kitchen table. She said that from now on she was recording all our conversations; she'd checked with her attorney, and anything I said would be admissible in court. Then she asked if I planned on molesting her again like I did last week.

I said, "I didn't molest you."

She said, "Lying under oath is a felony."

I said, "I just want to pick up Zoë and go."

She screamed and said, "Oh shit. You totally just hit me."

I said, "No, I didn't. What the fuck?"

She screamed again and punched herself in the face.

I went into the living room. Zoë was hiding under the table, crying.

I said, "I didn't hit Mommy."

The bathroom door opened. Ashram stepped out wearing a silk kimono. He had a samurai sword strapped to his waist. He said, "Dude, you better go."

I said, "But I'm supposed to babysit while you and Wendy see *The Da Vinci Code*."

He pulled the sword out of its sheath and said, "None of us wants trouble."

I said, "This is my family."

He said, "This is all being recorded. Everything. You're done."

When I got back to my apartment, I called Frank and said, "Do you have any more of those golden-brown rocks? I could really use some good dreams."

Frank said, "Sorry, dude. I don't do drugs anymore. I'm reading this book by J. Krishnamurti and praying without ceasing."

I said, "Don't believe a word the Highway Snakes tell you. Stick to your prayer. It'll pay off eventually."

We met at the Radio Lounge. I ordered an IPA, and Frank ordered a glass of water.

"OM," he said. "Shantih shantih shantih…"

"Frank," I said, snapping my fingers in front of his face. "I get it. Believe me, I get it. But I really need your undivided, non-praying attention for like five minutes."

Frank blinked and looked around. "Where are we?"

I said, "I need help. Wendy's boyfriend came at me with a sword. He's moving my family to Hawaii. There are tape recordings. None of it's true, but I wouldn't believe myself if I testified in court."

Frank asked if I'd ever done anything heroic. For instance: save kittens from a burning building? Volunteer at a homeless shelter?

I said, "This one time I found a dead snake on the side of the road in Utah and cut it open with a switchblade and freed its slithering babies."

Frank said, "Yeah, that's not gonna play well in court. What else?"

I thought about it. All I could come up with was being a dad. I was pretty good at that until Wendy said she didn't want to be married anymore. Then something went haywire in my brain, and ever since I'd been pretty unstable. Like the time I stole Zoë's allowance to buy hand rolling tobacco or the time I was too hung over to remember my pin number and we had to eat lunch at a soup kitchen.

I said, "I was a good dad for a while. I really was."

Frank looked down at his water glass and started praying.

Wendy and Ashram and Zoë got on an airplane and flew across the world to live on a smoldering volcano covered in cock-roaches and coconuts. For a few days I slept. When I woke up, I covered my head in a blanket and tried to reenter whatever dream I'd just arisen from, which, even when it was a nightmare, was still happier than my life. Mostly, it worked. I saw sunlight coming through my window. I blinked and it was night. I blinked and it was day.

But one day I got up to use the bathroom and didn't get back in bed. Instead, I walked around my apartment, picking up things Zoë left behind: a *Dora the Explorer* doll, a pink pair of OshKosh overalls, a 128-pack of colored markers. I put them in a cardboard box and stuffed it in the back of my closet and sat down on the floor and cried for a long time.

You probably want to hear all the sordid details from that darkest hour of my life. How I blacked out every night and puked and woke up without any will to live and took a Bear Bus back and forth to work all winter just to earn enough money to get fucked up again. But other things happened too. Incredible things. Because life isn't simple, and on the worst day of my life, I laughed so hard I cried, and then a beautiful woman invited me to her apartment, gave me a hand job in a bathtub full of eucalyptus oil, and the next morning played me a song on her violin—a tune I didn't recognize, but if I remember right was the most haunting, perfect melody I'd ever heard.

38

Lady Pain

Back in high school when I was a member of the Inevitable Death Society, before I tried to kill myself and accidentally wrote one of the greatest poems of all time, I wanted to be the guitarist for a grunge band. It was the reason I grew my hair long, the better to fall in my face as I strummed heavenly, distorted chords while some troubled friend of mine wailed in a microphone lyrics he'd scribbled on the back of a Goodwill receipt.

I guess it was inevitable that, having abandoned my dream of being a great writer, I decided to be a great musician instead.

I put an ad on the window of the Radio Lounge:

WANTED: Lead singer for grunge band. Good voice ideal, but bad voice okay. Must love Pearl Jam, RHCP, Kurt Vonnegut, cigarettes. Serious candidates only. 802-555-9482

The only person who replied to the ad was Frank. He came over and strummed his ukulele and sang an old-timey rendition of Public Enemy's "Don't Believe the Hype." He wasn't a good singer, but I let him join the band. We bought a bottle of Old Crow and started writing songs. All of them were about our ex-wives. There was "PMS Eyes," "Litter Box Letdown," "No Sex Forever," and my personal favorite, "Divorce Court." We named the band Lady Pain & the Vanquished Man-Babies.

I was Lady Pain. I'd wear Wendy's green cocktail dress and sing songs from the perspective of a hurtful wife. My band-mates, dressed only in diapers, would cower and accompany me.

Frank knew a drummer named Phil. He came over and auditioned. He was way too talented to play with a pair of embittered hacks like us, but he liked the idea of performing in a diaper and agreed to join the band.

Our first show was at a venue called the Roxy on Main Street. Phil knew the booking agent. He let us open for a local band called Wet Thesaurus. The show started at 9 p.m., but there were only six people in the audience: the members of Wet Thesaurus, Penelope, and Penelope's new boyfriend Huck. We waited as long as we could, hoping more people would show up, but two members of Wet Thesaurus went outside for a cigarette, and Lady Pain & the Vanquished Man-Babies made our world debut for an audience of four.

Frank had recently traded his ukulele for a broken sitar. He unrolled a Persian rug and sat with his legs twisted into a pretzel-shape and played an extended raga. The audience fidgeted. Huck cracked a PBR tall boy, which was oddly resonant in the empty concert hall. But as the raga came to an end, Phil hit his crash cymbal at the same moment I strummed a distorted G-chord, and we broke into a feverish rendition of "Litter Box Letdown."

I was wearing mascara and forced myself to cry as I performed, which was easy because my life was in shambles. The mascara ran down my cheeks and dried into pretty jellyfish shapes, which formed a nice contrast to my platinum blond wig and cherry red lipstick. I screamed and cried and missed a few chords and—just like the first time I had sex—blacked out. I didn't regain consciousness until we were two-thirds of the way into our set, playing a pared-down version of "Divorce Court." I looked up from my guitar just long enough to witness a sea of people who'd arrived early for Wet Thesaurus and were inadvertently witnessing what they must have assumed was drug-induced Kabuki theater.

When we finished our set, no one applauded. The audience just stood there with their mouths open, not drinking beer. Then Penelope screamed, "You guys are amazing!" and the audience decided that yes, whatever this was, it was amazing, and everyone cheered.

Since nobody was around for "Litter Box Letdown," we played an encore performance that transitioned into a new song called "Hawaii is a Very Bad Place," and then I sung an acapella version of "No Sex Forever," pausing occasionally when my sobbing got too overwhelming, and then I walked offstage and threw up into a waste basket.

People rushed the stage. They wanted to know what our band was called and how they could get our CD.

I said three of our songs were on MySpace and our album would be out in October or January or possibly never, and then I walked outside and lit a cigarette.

A mob of beautiful women surrounded me. They told me how talented and sexy I was in my dress and makeup.

I said, "Yeah, I know. I know."

Two of the women asked if they could go to bed with me. I said sure, and that night I rectified the mistake I made back in 1997 when I botched my first ménage à trois, but it didn't make me happy.

I woke up with two naked women next to me. We smoked cigarettes in bed and had sex again and then we went out to brunch together as a kind of post-coital family. I ordered the eggs benedict with a side of hash browns. When I pierced the yolk, the beautiful golden goo flowed all over my plate, but all I could think of was my daughter 6,000 miles away, eating pineapple and learning to surf. I wondered if she called Ashram "Dad." I wondered if she thought about me ever, and if so, I hoped she didn't hate me.

On a humid morning in August, Angela called and said she was in Burlington for an apocalypse conference, and would I be interested in meeting up for coffee and reminiscing about the old days? I said sure and 10 minutes later was sitting face to face with the second of three women who broke my heart.

Angela caught me up on the last six years of her life. She said that after I left the farm for Vermont, she fell in love with a survival skills instructor named Leonard. They got engaged and were busy planning their fire-and-brimstone-themed wedding when she caught him sending dick pics to his basketweaving instructor, Porcupine. Since then, she'd picked up the pieces and was avidly pursuing her deepest passion: preparing for Armageddon.

I told Angela about Zoë and my marriage and divorce and how I was dressing up as a woman now and performing rock and roll shows.

While I spoke, she looked at me with an expression I couldn't place: doe-eyed, interested, hanging on my every word.

"You seem different," she said.

"I *am* different," I said.

"No. Like, you're a completely different person."

"I am."

"But I mean like—not the same person at all."

As we were saying our goodbyes, I invited Angela to come to my show that night, Lady Pain's first headlining gig at the Radio Lounge.

Maybe it was because my old flame was in the audience, or because I was performing at that beautiful bar where I'd puked and cried and ruined my mind on a hundred occasions. Whatever it was, I achieved a magical state on stage that night. My eyes rolled back in their sockets and spirits entered me, and I flailed and cried and told the audience the story of my suffering. People stood up on the tables and cheered and laughed at my antics as I pantomimed stomping on my bandmates and ripping their hearts out of their sternums—an effect I achieved using a balled-up athletic sock dipped in red wine.

After the last song ended, I dropped my guitar and ran outside. A mob of beautiful women surrounded me and asked if they could go to bed with me. Before I could answer, Angela came outside and chased them away. We went upstairs.

She said, "Will you put your penis inside of me without a condom?"

I said, "Sure."

I put my penis inside of her. It was strange and sort of lovely, but something felt off. I thought of Montana and how I'd wanted nothing more in the world than to make a baby with this crazy woman who thought the world was going to end any minute, and then I thought of Zoë screaming for two years nonstop. I imagined making a baby with Angela.

I said, "Actually, this is making me uncomfortable."

She said, "I thought this is what you always wanted."

I said, "I don't know what I want anymore."

I went to the bathroom and washed my makeup off and looked down at my penis. It was so pathetic with its white shaft with blue veins and strawberry head where Mom and Dad had my foreskin surgically removed when I was a baby. I thought of everything I'd gone through to put it inside Angela. Now that we'd done it, I just wanted to live in a cabin at 3,000 feet, reading the American Transcendentalists.

39

Tiresias

A few days later Angela returned to Portland, and we started emailing each other. We decided we were star-crossed lovers who kept missing each other by not being in love at the same time, a situation we were finally in a place to rectify now that we were old and ridiculous and nobody else wanted us.

I emailed Angela long love letters with references to William Blake, Eddie Vedder, and the Upanishads. She emailed me links to YouTube videos on how to gut a wild boar.

"Please watch this and take notes," she said. "It's going to be important to know this stuff when the Horned Lamb opens the Seventh Seal."

I was reluctant to watch those videos. I loved animals. I didn't want to gut any animal, let alone a fuzzy one with tusks, but Angela kept sending me naked selfies and not-so-subtle innuendos that after all this time it was me, nervous Kevin, who would join her as her celestial spouse in the End of Days.

Reluctantly, I watched the video. It was disgusting. While most animals are pleasant to look at on the outside, their insides are full of pink intestines and yellow connective tissue that are clearly never meant to see the light of day. I decided right then to become a vegetarian, and if the day came when God asked me to prove my fitness for his Kingdom, I'd forfeit at the outset and join my friends in hell.

Since Angela lived 3,000 miles away, I had to make do with dirty talk and a steady stream of naked selfies.

She said, "I hope you know I'm only doing this because you're going to marry me one day and be my sacred warrior husband."

I said, "Yeah, of course," but I didn't know what that meant. Were Angela and I engaged? Had I participated in an ancient marriage ritual when I thought we were just doing our horoscopes and burning candles in honor of our elders?

She said we needed to consecrate our Astral Matrimony by visiting the Oracle of Delphi in Ancient Greece.

I didn't know what was real, so I said, "Does this involve getting on an airplane or reading a book?"

She said, "Airplane."

I said, "Here's the thing. Not all artists have trust funds; some of us have to work at teddy bear factories."

Angela said, "I have a trust fund. A big one. You don't need to worry about money anymore."

I couldn't believe it. After all this time, I'd found my benefactor. Now I could live the life I'd always dreamed of, spending my days sitting around writing essays about how money was the root of unhappiness.

We got on an airplane and flew to Athens and rented a car. I didn't know how to drive a stick, so Angela drove. We fought the whole time.

Angela said, "A real man would know how to drive a stick."

I said, "I'm not a real man. In fact, as of a few days ago, I spent 30 percent of my time dressed as a woman."

Angela told me to get in the driver's seat and lectured me about the finer points of operating a manual transmission.

I said no problem and stepped on the gas, which turned out to be the clutch. The car lurched, and a dozen Europeans whizzed by, waving their fists and cursing me in Greek.

Angela gave up and took the wheel and drove in an aggressive manner, passing all the drivers who'd passed me.

She said, "How are we supposed to survive the apocalypse if you can't tell the difference between the clutch and the gas pedal?"

I said, "Do you think there will only be manual transmissions when the world ends?"

Angela said, "That's not the point," and for the rest of the drive refused to speak to me.

The Oracle of Delphi wasn't an actual oracle but a pile of rocks on an orange hill with a thousand tourists walking around wearing fanny packs and headsets that asked them to imagine it was the year 600 B.C.

We joined a tour led by an elderly British man in a tweed sportscoat. He pointed his cane at a circle of rocks and told us to close our eyes and pretend it was a temple.

"Citizens used to come from all over Greece to ask for guidance and wisdom from the priestess," he said. "History tells us that Pythia's hallucinations were the result of toxic vapors her assistants pumped through a vent in the floor."

Angela laughed. "That's some bullshit."

"Excuse me?" asked the tour guide.

"Vapors?" Angela shook her head. "Next thing you're going to say astrology isn't real."

"It's well documented—"

"SCIENCE!" said Angela, waving her fingers around like everything coming out of the tour guide's mouth was mumbo jumbo.

We got back in the rental car and zoomed west toward the Ionian Islands where Angela had booked us a week at a fancy hotel paid for by dividends from her father's timber company.

"I bet that tour guide's never sprinkled menstrual blood on his crops during a full moon," said Angela, shaking her head.

"Probably not," I agreed.

"Men are scared of powerful women."

I nodded my head vigorously. It was the first true thing Angela had said all day.

Our hotel, Apollo Suites, was on the island of Kefalonia. It was new construction built to resemble an ancient temple. There were statues of Zeus and Hera in our room on opposite sides of the bed, staring at us. On the ceiling was a mosaic of a giant owl with enormous yellow eyes.

Angela and I tried to have sex with all those gods staring at us, but I got intimidated and forgot how to move my hips forward and backward.

Angela got testy and said that her ex-boyfriend Leonard always knew what to do with his hips.

"He looked like Hugh Jackman as the Wolverine," she said, touching herself. "His mutton chops were the size of actual mutton chops. His pecs were like full moons."

I looked in the mirror. I didn't look like Wolverine. More like a sickly child Wolverine saved from the Brotherhood of Mutants.

Angela described all the things Leonard used to do to give her multiple orgasms. I tried to replicate his maneuvers, but Angela said I was doing it wrong.

"No, like this," she said, pushing two fingers into an imaginary vagina, making a come-hither gesture.

I tried again, but every time I touched what I thought was her G-spot, she flinched like I was electrocuting her with a cattle prod.

"Never mind," she said, reaching for her vibrator.

Angela was right. I couldn't gut a wild boar. I was an imposter. I'd made false promises because I thought I was in love with her, but actually I was in love with Wendy, and now I was in Greece.

I went outside and lit a cigarette, and the goddess Athena flew down out of the sky in the form of an owl.

She perched on the banister and said, "Hey there."

"Hi, Athena," I said.

"How do you like Greece?"

"It's okay. I don't know. Apparently, I'm bad at sex."

"Do you want me to transform you into a lusty goat?"

"Nah, I'm good."

Athena told me about Tiresias, the prophet who got turned into a woman for seven years and later got turned back into a man.

I said, "Yeah, I did that too."

She said, "He communicated with the dead to foretell the future."

I said, "I often wish I was dead."

Athena said that ancient history was full of freaks who amounted to more than their gender-stable counterparts and that if Angela shamed me for not meeting some masculine ideal, that was her problem, not mine.

"I guess," I said.

Athena wished me luck on my journey and flew away. I went back inside. Angela was in her nightgown, reading *The Rainbow* by D.H. Lawrence.

"We never finished this," she said.

"You're right," I said.

I crawled into bed and rested my head on her stomach like a baby.

40

The Hairy Monster

When I got home from Greece, I quit my band and moved across the country to live with Angela in her 2,000-square-foot Craftsman home in Northeast Portland. We only had sex when Angela was ovulating. The idea was to populate the post-apocalyptic earth with red-headed babies who hopefully inherited their mom's personality and survival skills and as few of their dad's weak genes as possible.

Every night, Angela dipped her fingers in her underwear and tested the viscosity of her vaginal mucous.

"It's time," she said.

She got on all fours and told me to get it over with as quickly as possible, but when I finished, not to pull out right away.

"Let it really seep in," she said. "I don't want any drops running down your leg. Got it?"

"Yes," I said.

"Yes, what?"

"Yes, ma'am," I said.

I started moving in and out, but it just depressed me.

"Can we stop and talk?" I asked.

"God. What now?"

I lit a cigarette and told Angela it was important to me to feel connected during sex.

"If you want to feel connected, quit looking at me like that."

"Like what?" I asked.

"Like you're stunned to be having sex with me."

Of course, I was. I was stunned to be having sex with anyone but my wife. Stunned to be having sex with anyone at all. The miracle of intercourse had never been lost on me; the 16-year-old version of me was always lurking in there somewhere, watching everything I did, pimple-covered, half a bowl of Cinnamon Toast Crunch in his braces, jerking off at the sexy parts.

At night, Angela's uterus throbbed. She wanted babies, ideally four or five years ago, but now would have to do. She consulted a fertility specialist who put me on a strict diet of raw oysters and ginseng supplements. I wasn't allowed to take hot baths or wear tight-fitting underwear, and my cigarette ration was cut to two a day.

Every 30 minutes, Angela put a thermometer under her tongue and took a finger-swipe of her vaginal mucous.

"My temp's a little high," she said. "And my mucous is medium viscous. Interesting."

"What do you want to do?" I asked.

"I want you to mount me," she said. "Just in case."

She leaned over the bed, pulled down her pants, and opened the book she was reading—Cormac McCarthy's *The Road*. While I went about my business, Angela read about post-apocalyptic shopping carts and cannibal zombies starving in an ash-covered world.

When I came, she said, "Oh hey, I booked our wedding venue. It's a vineyard in McMinnville called Maplewood Estates.

There's an orchard and this giant oak tree that got struck by lightning. We can have our ceremony under the tree. At first, I was thinking we should get married by a priest, but lately I'm leaning toward a witch."

I said, "Wendy and I got married by a witch."

She said, "A warlock, then. Ooooooh! I want to show you the wedding dresses I've been looking at!"

Angela sat with her legs up in the air to prevent my semen from dripping out of her and pulled up a website on her laptop.

"What do you think of these?" she asked.

The dresses were pretty, but I wasn't sure I was ready to get married. For one thing, due to a prescribed waiting period in the state of Vermont, I was still technically married to Wendy, and also in love with her and hadn't bought Angela an engagement ring or asked her to be my wife.

But instead of suggesting we slow down and make sure we were compatible enough to spend the rest of our lives together, I said, "I like the vintage one. We'll have banjo players and a violinist. It'll be a hoedown."

We ordered invitations and registered on Crate & Barrel. As our wedding day approached, Angela started obsessing over my grooming habits.

"Shave here and here," she said. "But not here."

I went along with it because I'd spent my whole life deferring to other people, in particular women who raised their voice when they got mad at me. I wasn't about to start making my own decisions now.

But a few days later, I looked in the mirror and discovered a hideous pair of mutton chops on my face. I'd been duped! Some of Angela's other eccentricities revealed themselves, and it became clear they were all part of a conscious effort to transform me into a crime-fighting beast. Like her request that I stop clipping my fingernails, or her profound disappointment when she inquired about my spirit animal, and I answered that I've always felt a magical kinship with the donkey.

"Not a wolverine?" she asked.

I laughed and her face turned red, and the next time she was ovulating, she wouldn't have sex with me until I growled at her.

One day I'd had enough of Angela's freaky business; I shaved off my sideburns, put on lipstick, and pranced about the house in a girlish manner that seemed closer to my authentic self than the masculine game she had me playing.

Angela was disgusted. She said Leonard never shaved his mutton chops or pranced around the house in a girlish manner. He walked upright and clawed her back during sex and gave her mind-blowing cunnilingus.

I said, "Why don't you marry Leonard then?"

Angela said, "He cheated on me. Also, he didn't believe in the apocalypse. He said we're all going to die from old age."

Angela burst into tears. I tried to comfort her, but when I went to put my arm around her, I accidentally elbowed her in the temple and gave her a black eye.

The next morning, I went downstairs to make coffee and found Angela sitting at the kitchen table, holding a mug of tea. Her eyes were red-rimmed, her jaw clenched. It was an expression I hadn't seen in three months of dating: pain mixed with inevitability, like a child about to rip the wings off a butterfly.

When she finally spoke, instead of saying hurtful things about my personality, she told me that she loved me.

I said, "I know I know I know I know," and started packing my things. I'd done this all before. I was good at it now.

I didn't know where to go, so I moved back in with my parents. They put me in my childhood bedroom with Samantha, Kirsten, Felicity, and a post-surgical Molly with hand-sewn scars where Wendy once pierced her with a dozen fondue skewers.

My dad asked what I planned on doing for work.

I said, "Angela has a trust fund, so I'm all set for money."

He said, "Didn't she break up with you?"

I said, "Oh shit, you're right."

My dad said that a friend of his owned a marketing-PR company in the suburbs. They had an opening at an entry-level position. Was I interested?

I said sure. I didn't care. A few days later I interviewed with them and never left.

PART V
THE LITTLE CLOD OF EARTH

Epilogue

Phoenix (née Wendy) and I worked out an agreement where Zoë got to spend her summers and holidays with me in Oregon. We ate at food carts, went ice skating at the Lloyd Center, and watched psychedelic clowns ride up and down Alberta Street on their tall bikes. Then I put her on a plane back to Hawaii and resumed my lonely life in the city, building websites by day, reading alone in bars at night.

In 2012, Zoë celebrated her 10th birthday. The celebration was at Richardson Ocean Park just east of Hilo, Hawaii, the city where Phoenix has been living all these years. I had a little extra money from my tax returns, so I bought a plane ticket and flew 2,500 miles to be there.

For an hour and a half, Zoë and all her tan friends splashed in the ocean, riding boogie boards and crowding around giant sea turtles. Zoë stayed in the water longer than her friends. She was blue when she got out. Shivering. Just like her mother.

The lucky devils ran dripping to a picnic table where Phoenix had paper plates and tofu dogs waiting for them. The kids gobbled up their make-believe meat with sandy fingers, and then we all sang "Happy Birthday."

Phoenix made Zoë's cake from scratch. The top was slanted, and the frosting looked like it had been put on by an overzealous toddler, but Zoë was happy as hell and I had to admit that for all her faults, Phoenix was a pretty good mom.

The next morning, I was sitting on the veranda of Phoenix and Ashram's house, eating cereal. They let me stay in the guest room, an arrangement none of us found awkward.

I was watching the frantic movements of a gecko running up and down a pillar when Zoë, hungover from her slumber party, stumbled outside and blinked as though she couldn't remember why I was there.

"Hey, Bug," I said.

"Hi, Dad," she said.

She sat down next to me, and in a rare moment of unprompted affection, wrapped her arms around me and rested her head on my shoulder.

"Late night?" I asked.

She nodded.

"How many slices of cake did you eat?"

She held up four fingers.

"Dear God."

The gecko darted up the side of the house suddenly, just barely escaping Humphrey's diabolical claws.

"Can I ask you a question?" asked Zoë.

"Go for it," I said.

"Why did you dress up as a woman when I was little?"

It wasn't the question I was expecting. After a few seconds, I said, "I was going through a hard time."

Zoë didn't respond, but her silence suggested what a pitiful answer this was.

"I guess I just wanted to know what it felt like," I said. "To be a woman."

She nodded. This answer satisfied her. Or at least, she gave me a kiss on the cheek and left the veranda for the kitchen, where she plopped down at a table with two of her best friends, similarly nursing sugar headaches.

Phoenix walked outside. She'd cut her hair short. She was pregnant.

"It's so nice to have you here," she said.

"Thanks for letting me stay with you," I said.

Humphrey hopped in my lap. I patted the spot at the base of his tail. He purred and rammed his face into my leg.

"You have a nice life," I said.

"It's pretty incredible," said Phoenix. "I mean… you could always move here."

"It's tempting."

I lit a cigarette. Phoenix peeked to make sure no one was looking and asked if she could have a drag. I handed it to her. She took the smoke deep into her lungs and smiled.

"Ashram's a good guy," I said.

"He's awesome, isn't he?"

We sat there for a few minutes, not saying anything. Eventually Phoenix got up and went into the house and started washing the heaping pile of birthday dishes. I finished my cigarette and went inside to help her.

I was in Hawaii a full week but only stayed with Phoenix and Ashram a couple days. When Zoë went back to school on Monday, I borrowed Ashram's bike, secured my backpack and tent to the tire rack, and went riding toward Kīlauea, the volcano that has been erupting more or less nonstop since 1983.

A few miles south of Hilo the trees closed in around me. I was riding through a tunnel of translucent green vegetation and violent animal sounds—squawking birds, creeping lizards, ribbiting frogs. Then I shot out the other side of the tunnel; the sky turned blue, and a lone white pillar of smoke appeared, rising from the coastline, the point where a finger of lava poured into the ocean.

I camped on the beach for a few days and met all kinds of wild people. There was a woman named "Dolphin Lady" who wore a wetsuit everywhere she went and swam with dolphins and said she once had a religious experience pressing her face against the gaping eye of a humpback whale. There were surfers who barely spoke but spent the entire day dialoguing with the ocean in a language I couldn't understand. And there were hippies sitting on tapestries laid out over the black sand, strumming Grateful Dead songs on their acoustic guitars.

I saw that life would be good here. I'd buy a small plot of land and grow ginger and finally learn how to ride a motorcycle. Every night at sunset, I'd ride God's pineapple highway, popping wheelies in front of volcanoes, while all around me, majestic surfers floated on top of the ocean like olive-skinned gods.

But for some reason, when the last day of my vacation came, I said goodbye to Phoenix and Ashram and Zoë and boarded my airplane. I returned to work and sat down at my desk and went back to building websites for healthcare organizations, just like before.

Now I'm sitting here in a field of Queen Anne's lace adjacent to a business park, waiting for something to happen. The sky is yellow and sooty. There are wildfires burning east of here. I feel fragile, like anything can happen. Zoë's not a kid anymore. She'll be a freshman this fall at the University of Hawai'i at Mānoa. I haven't heard a song that made me feel scared and alive in years. Am I too old to move to the desert and start over again from the beginning?

I keep coming back to the same memory: 1998, sitting in the passenger seat of Angela's pickup, cresting the Rockies, drifting into the sublime mystery of Montana. When I rolled down the window for the first time and stuck my head out and took a sniff—that smell. Grass and wildflowers and God knows what. Overabundance. The magic and stupidity of youth, not understanding what I'd gotten myself into. That whole drive Angela was talking about the end of the world, but I understand now that she was really talking about her fear of meaninglessness. That everything can be ripped away in a second, and if that happens, why should we keep trying?

I'm not sure I have the answer. I don't think anybody does. But here I am at the precipice again. Any second—I can feel it—somebody's going to roll down their window and ask if I want to go to New Orleans or Detroit or Albuquerque. To roll out of this life and into another one, and all these years later, I just want to be stupid again. To say yes, yes, yes. I don't care where. Let's go.

Acknowledgements

Huge, unbounded gratitude to: Aaron Burch, Brett Gregory, Brian Alan Ellis, Bud Smith, Chelsea Hodson, Chelsea Martin, Derrick Martin-Campbell, Eric Arndt, Joey & Mik Grantham, Julia Dixon Evans, Juliet Escoria, Kate Jayroe, Matt Sailor, Morgan Black, Patrick Wensink, Piers Rippey, Santi Elijah Holley, and the entire Maloney/Garrett/Hōlpus fam. Enormous thanks to Asia Atuah for your invaluable edits. This book wouldn't exist without Eric Obenauf and Eliza Wood-Obenauf, making magic in Columbus, Ohio. All my love forever and ever to Lud, Musi, Turkey, Fennel Fox, and my amazing wife, Aubrey Lenahan.

Notes

On pages 3 and 61, the phrases "sing the body electric" and "sound my barbaric yawp over the roofs of the world" are borrowed from poems included in the 1855 poetry collection *Leaves of Grass* by Walt Whitman, the former phrase appearing in "I Sing the Body Electric" and the latter appearing in "Song of Myself."

Page 20 contains a reference to Richard Brautigan's poem "All Watched Over by Machines of Loving Grace" from the 1967 collection of the same name.

Lyrics from the 1991 Red Hot Chili Peppers song "Under the Bridge" are referenced on page 22.

A quote from Henry David Thoreau's 1854 novel *Walden* appears on page 25.

Page 25 contains both a quote from Henry Miller's 1934 novel *Tropic of Cancer* and a quote from *Gandhi: His Life and Message for the World*, a 1950 biography of Mahatma Gandhi by Louis Fischer.

Pages 82, 83, 114, and 187 reference lines from Allen Ginsberg's poem "Howl," published in his 1956 poetry collection *Howl and Other Poems*.

Two Dollar Radio

Books too loud to Ignore

ALSO AVAILABLE Here are some other titles you might want to dig into.

BORN INTO THIS STORIES BY ADAM THOMPSON

→ The Story Prize Spotlight Award, Winner.
→ Readings Prize for New Australian Fiction, Shortlist.
→ Age Book of the Year award, Finalist.
→ Queensland Literary Awards – University of Southern Queensland Steele Rudd Award for a Short Story Collection, Shortlist.

← "With its wit, intelligence and restless exploration of the parameters of race and place, Thompson's debut collection is a welcome addition to the canon of Indigenous Australian writers." —Thuy On, *The Guardian*

ALLIGATOR STORIES BY DIMA ALZAYAT

→ PEN/Robert W. Bingham Award, Finalist.
→ Swansea University Dylan Thomas Prize 2021, Finalist.
→ James Tait Black Memorial Prize, Finalist.
→ Short Story Prize, Longlist.
→ Arab American Book Awards, Honorable Mention.

← "The richly detailed short fictions in this debut from a Damascus-born scribe form an intricate, breathtaking mosaic of modern Muslim life." —Michelle Hart, *O, The Oprah Magazine*

THEY CAN'T KILL US UNTIL THEY KILL US ESSAYS BY HANIF ABDURRAQIB

→ Best Books 2017: NPR, *Rolling Stone, Buzzfeed, Paste Magazine, Esquire, Chicago Tribune, Vol. 1 Brooklyn, Entropy, Heavy, Book Riot,* among others.

← "A much-needed collection for our time. [Abdurraqib] has proven to be one of the most essential voices of his generation." —Juan Vidal, NPR

← "A collection of death-defying protest songs for the Black Lives Matter era." —Walton Muyumba, *Chicago Tribune*

WHITE DIALOGUES STORIES BY BENNETT SIMS

→ Winner of the Rome Prize for Literature 2018-19.

← "One of the most genuinely terrifying, brilliant short story collections of the past decade. These stories are so smart and so unsettling; every sentence will unnerve you. He's kind of like if Alfred Hitchcock and Brian Evenson raised a baby with David Foster Wallace and Nicholson Baker. Sims should be a household name in horror." —Carmen Maria Machado, *Lit Hub*

NIGHT ROOMS ESSAYS BY GINA NUTT

→ "A Best Book of 2021" —NPR

← "In writing both revelatory and intimate, Nutt probes the most frightening aspects of life in such a way that she manages to shed light and offer understanding even about those things that lurk in the deepest and darkest of shadows." —Kristin Iversen, *Refinery29*

← "A hallucinatory experience that doesn't obscure but instead deepens the subjects that Nutt explores." —Jeannie Vanasco, *The Believer*